Punished

CALAVERA HOTELS
BOOK ONE

NIX MURGUIA

Content Warnings

Punished is a dark cartel romance and a work of fiction made for your smut pleasure. The author does not condone any situations or actions that take place between these characters. Proceed to the prologue if you prefer to go in blindly otherwise please go over the trigger warnings below.

Trigger warnings include but are not limited to: Graphic Violence, drug/alcohol use, addiction, Non/Dub Con, CNC, torture, bondage, somnophilia, erotic asphyxiation, rape/sexual assault (not features but mentioned), and kidnapping.

Playlist

Diosa - Myke Towers

Me Metí En El Ruedo -Luis R Conriquez

Por Tu Maldito Amor - Vicente Fernández

Back On My BS - BigXthaPlug

Fuentes de Ortiz - Peso Pluma

El Gordo Trae El Mando - Chino Pacas

Sucker for Pain - Lil Wayne, Wiz Khalifa, Imagine Dragons

Ando - Jere Klein, Gittobeatz

Amor Tumbado - Nathanel Cano

No Mienten - Becky G

Sad Girl - Lana Del Rey

Only One - Jessie Reyez

Ocean Remix - Karol G, Jessie Reyez

Contents

Prologue

Adrian

Bryan: Hit me up. I'll send you my location.

Adrian: Okay. I'll be there in 40 minutes. I'm dropping Diana off.

I drive up to the large estate where Diana lives and park. We've been fighting as usual, and in true Diana fashion, I already expect her to get out and slam the door. To my surprise, she turns to me and kisses me. She kisses me long and hard, pulling me closer to her, her hands around my neck. My tongue slides to find hers as she moans in my mouth. Diana has always been a good fuck. Nothing more and nothing less. She probably knows that deep down, which is why we fight so much. She wants obsession and devotion, and at seventeen, I can't offer her either of those things.

She pulls away, panting, when an outside light comes on. Daddy Dearest, Judge Julian Nunez, stands out on the porch, and judging by the look on his face, he is more than pissed at seeing his sweet, innocent daughter outside with a lowlife like me. She kisses me one last time before she exits the car. I give an award-winning 'fuck you' smile to Julian before I make my way to the Second Ward of Houston to pick up my homeboy, Efren.

Efren has always been my most loyal friend. He knows about my life, but never tries to pry or ask questions. He knows my motives and I know his. Do we like the shit we have to do to survive? No. But we didn't choose this life. It was merely the only path available for us to get ahead. Efren comes out in a striped green and black polo, his hair slicked back and a cigarette behind his ear.

"What's the pretty boy want?" he says as he slides into the front seat, and I know he's referring to Bryan. He often warns me about Bryan, but I need to keep our connections to Saint Rita's. The Private Catholic High School is where most of our profit comes from. A part of me loves to see all those posh kids strung out on drugs. Blowing all their parents' money to get their fix. The same parents who look down on me, like Diana's dad. The parents crying as they put their

kids in high-end rehabs none of us could ever afford. They are fucked up like me, with my mother's addiction ruining what remained of her. Her addiction and neglect created a monster in me. Her addiction should have been the one reason to discourage me from making narcotics my full-time job, but instead, it fuels it. There has always been something in me that thought if I climbed to the top of this world that I could find where my mom was getting her fix from and cut it all off. That part of me is delusional because I know once you make it in the streets, the only way out is death.

Efren and I arrive at the location Bryan sent us. It's some type of playground in the suburbs of Houston. Bryan is wearing all black, hiding under the hood of his sweatshirt when we walk up. He's always paranoid about getting caught. Like a fucking pussy. I approach him and he hands me the money. I give it to Efren to count before handing Bryan the few grams he asked for.

Faster than I can blink, I hear sirens as Bryan takes off running. I run to get in my car, Efren following behind me.

"What the fuck was that?" he says, and I try to take off, but two cop cars cage me in. Efren and I know this drill too well, so we step out, hands behind our heads and lower to our knees. Efren stares coldly into the cop's eyes as he spits on the ground. They are immediately on top of us, forcing us to the ground and handcuffing both of us. They start to search *the car and ironically find over 500 grams of cocaine in my trunk and a suitcase of money. Neither of which are mine.*

Diana would later stare straight at me and testify that she was with me and Efren. She claimed that we kept dropping by random houses and coming out with money. The prosecutor used my phone records to trap Bryan, but his family had money and he had an alibi, so the case was thrown out. Efren and I honored the street code and refused to snitch, but I was buying time until I saw him again.

Our shitty court-appointed lawyer pushed to lower the sentence, but it didn't help that our judge and the prosecutor were Julian Nunez's golfing buddies. I was fucked from every side of the judicial system. I had no fucking chance from the get-go. Bryan clearly set it up, and I was going to find out why. As soon as I leave this prison, I will find everyone who plotted against us, and I will punish each and every one of them.

Chapter One

Mireya

We are halfway through the movie when I look down at his cell to see a new text message.

Diana: I'll be there to pick you up.

I want to ask who Diana is, but immediately know better. He gets up from my bed and starts looking for his clothes before texting back. Diana was most likely his newest side piece. In my head, I start going through all the Dianas from Saint Rita's, as Bryan ties his shoes. When he leaves, I can start the downward spiral of comparing myself and bringing all my insecurities and childhood trauma back to the surface. He looks at me and I reach for his hand. I hate it when he leaves. He never stays long after he gets what he wants from me. He pulls away and looks back down at his phone. His face softens, and he puts on that smile he uses when he needs something from me. A smile that makes me feel like he loves me, like I am valuable to him.

"If anyone asks you, I was here with you all night. Do you understand me?" I nod.

"I'm serious, Mireya. The cops are going to question you, and I need to know I can trust you." He strokes my cheek and leans down to kiss me.

"I will tell them you were with me all night."

And I had without question. Bryan had snuck back into my bedroom early that morning and the cops followed shortly after. I told them he had been with me all night, and I stuck to that story, even when the prosecutor tried to dig up evidence on him. What I didn't know was that Adrian had also been involved. Thankfully, my age at the time guaranteed my identity would remain anonymous, and Bryan had walked free from any charges. I never had to face Adrian, but I read up on his case, and I felt guilty that he had been convicted. The Diana who was texting Bryan was Adrian's girlfriend at the time, so I knew right away that something was off about the entire situation.

I had wanted to ask Bryan what he was doing that required an alibi, but Bryan Mendez is not the type of person you ask questions of. I often look back at that memory and wonder how I hadn't seen the signs that I was being manipulated. Bryan was abusive and controlling, but I still found a way to convince myself that he loved me. I had spent the majority of my life delusional about love. Starting with Adrian.

Adrian Ibarra was the first boy to show any interest in me. We were fourteen the first time he walked me home from the bus stop. Our mothers had been friends, but he never paid me much attention. No one in our neighborhood did. I was often shy, and isolated myself from people, insecure about my weight, glasses, and braces. My mom would make it her daily mission to remind me that I was ugly.

"You look just like your dad's family. Fat and ugly," she would say every morning after my father left for work. She would never say it in front of him. My father let her live with us, but he could barely stand her commentaries about him and his family. I never understood why they stayed together, but my father made it up to me. He treated me like I deserved the world at my feet.

But my mother's words rang true. I was not the girl guys were drawn to, but Adrian was the boy all the middle school girls were in love with. Over time, the after-school walks turned into walking me to classes, or letting me ride on his bike pegs with my arms wrapped around his shoulders. The first time he grabbed my hand, I thought it was a joke. Maybe one of his friends dared him to do it. Everyone in school laughed at me, but Adrian never cared what other people thought. He never stopped holding my hand, and slowly, all his time and attention was on me. It was puppy love, but it always felt real. Little did I know he would break my heart the summer before my freshman year. The same year my father died.

A few months after he broke up with me, my father had a heart attack and my mother's mental and verbal abuse got worse. I took my tia Vicky's offer to stay with her in Arizona until she could pull some strings to get me into Saint Rita's. She had worked the majority of her life for Calavera Hotels in Arizona for Don Fernando and had her connections to the Houston location.

I was enrolled halfway through my freshmen year, and after losing some weight, growing boobs, and a much needed glow up, I found my way right into Bryan's arms. I was the new girl at Saint Rita's, and there was no trace of Mireya-see-ya-later from our little barrio.

I had to go back with my mother, who, at that point, was a bitter shell of a person. She not only resented my father the whole time they were married, but also his entire family. When she found out Tia Vicky had pulled some strings and helped me to get myself back on track, she was even more resentful.

She never worked a day in her life, and the money my father left us was spent on designer clothing to impress the different men she would search for in the high-end Houston clubs. There were many times I was worried the lights were going to get turned off at home. I told Bryan about it, and he used money to secure my devotion to him. Showing up with wads of cash, looking for a warm place to bury his cock at night. With my mom gone, he had a safe place to crash while he was drunk and high.

I'm not sure any of the other girls at Saint Rita's wanted to deal with his instability. I was desperate to survive, so I found comfort in the dysfunction. I knew Bryan wasn't a saint. Shit, deep down, I also knew he didn't love me, but I'd settle for being needed if it got me out of this house.

All I ever wanted was to be loved, and if it wasn't for that night, I'd probably still be content being whatever I was to him. I'm still lost in the thought when I finally pull my attention back to the source of what triggered my flashback.

I look down at the purple and gold invitation in my hands.

MR. & MRS. JULIAN NUNEZ
INVITE YOU TO JOIN THEM TO
CELEBRATE THE ENGAGEMENT
OF THEIR DAUGHTER

Diana Nunez
TO
Bryan Mendez

"Can you also let Mr. Consuelo know that Mrs. Nunez is adamant the party décor matches this invitation?" I look up to meet the party planner's sharp eyes. She's been rambling on about what her vision was for the party.

I had forgotten Bryan and Diana's engagement party was to be held here at Calavera Hotels. I look at the date–June 21st. I would hopefully be starting my nursing practicum with Doctor Aguilar and wouldn't have to see them parading around in front of me. But what if I had to see them before then? My anxiety spikes. How was I going to watch Bryan and Diana laughing and in love while I just barely threw away the last reminder of him a few months ago? What sick joke was the universe playing on me?

"Yes, that's not a problem. I will take this up to Enrique."

The invitation sits in my shaky hand. After Bryan and I broke up and our lights got turned off for real, Tia Vicky pulled her strings again and got me a job here at Calavera Hotels. The Consuelos created a work atmosphere that felt more like family than anything else, so I enjoyed my job working at the front desk. It also was how I found my best friends, Thalia and Alma.

I watch the party planner exit through the large revolving doors and check to see if there are any guests needing help before I make my way up the stairs to Enrique's office.

Enrique Consuelo is the youngest of the Consuelo brothers and the best looking. Rumors have it he originally gave up his inheritance when Vicente Consuelo disowned him when he came out as gay. He took a modeling job in California and became one of the top influencers at the peak of social media. It wasn't until the oldest brother, Ivan, died a few years ago that Enrique returned. The prodigal son, who now sits as the Event Coordinator of Calavera Hotels. Pretty much a hobby for him, considering how much stock he already has in the three hotels that spread across the West Coast.

Don Vicente is the head of the Consuelo Family. I've

watched many of his earlier interviews recounting the story of how he and his two brothers, Fernando and Rogelio, started their legacy. They credit their younger sister, Maite, who would draw in soldiers traveling through Mexico with her cooking. Most people, my mother included, say that she was a prostitute, but Don Vicente laughs at the accusations. According to the legend, many of the soldiers left her with valuable treasures, and one soldier asked her to watch after a large sum of gold. When he didn't return after several years, the Consuelo family would use that money to set up their own legacy.

I knock on the door to Enrique's office, but I hear another familiar voice. When the door opens, I meet green eyes and a soft smile. Patricio Consuelo. Don Vicente's middle son. He stands at six-foot-six, and his body is chiseled to perfection. Women are constantly throwing themselves at him. Many would line up just to watch him on the days he worked out in the hotel gym. Thalia even caught me watching him one day through the window and threatened to gouge my eyes out. Thalia was Ivan's biological daughter, but Patricio was more of a father to her than he ever was.

"Mireya, come on in," Patricio says, arms extending to the large office space. Enrique's ear is glued to the phone. He looks annoyed as he looks at me, but that's not uncommon for Enrique. Just my breathing alone at times has distressed him. His eyes narrow, and I can feel him already judging my attire. I'm wearing black pants and the signature black polo with a Calavera Hotel logo on the upper left side. Even in a uniform of his choosing, I have somehow committed a fashion mistake, I'm sure. He ends the call then looks up to me, brows high, waiting to see why I have disturbed him with my presence.

"The Nunez party planner wants to make sure that the décor matches the invitation," I say quickly and out of breath. Patricio's smile fades as he turns from me to Enrique.

"The Nunez family?! As in Judge Julian Nunez?!!!" Enrique just looks at Patricio. Patricio slams his hands on the desk.

"The Nunez family? What the fuck are they going to be doing here, Enrique?"

Enrique rolls his eyes and sighs. "I don't owe you an explanation, Patricio, but I did inform you months ago that he booked his daughter's engagement party here. He is a close friend of the family."

I can tell they are about to get into a heated argument, so I turn to leave, but I stop outside the door when I hear a familiar name.

"He *was* a friend of our family, but you know damn well

he had his part in locking Adrian up."

Adrian. My Adrian?

"Adrian is getting out of prison soon, and he will be staying in one of the penthouses," Patricio says. I continue down the hallway and back down the steps as their arguing continues. My mind is a mess, trying to process the information.

Adrian.

Coming *home?*

My heart feels like it's going to explode.

This can't be real. First Bryan and now Adrian. The universe for sure was delighting in the twisted joke that was now my life.

Chapter Two

Patricio

I'm sitting in the dark-lit area of the Hotel restaurant. This is usually the place where I handle any outside business. I'm waiting for my *socio* Ignacio Fernandez, better known as Conejo. One of the deadliest sicarios on this side of the Houston-Mexico Border, and my right-hand man. As a former cartel hitman, he is loyal and trustworthy when it comes to the tainted side of my business dealings.

For the last three years, my nephew, Adrian, has been helping Conejo to form an alliance with Los Antros, a powerful prison gang within Houston's Federal Detention Center. In order to provide our men going in security in the FDC, we need to have an alliance. It is hard to get into Los Antros, and Ivan's reputation was the only thing we had to benefit us when Adrian approached them. He was our ticket in.

I put off looking for Adrian after he was born. After his mother, Soledad, begged me to leave them alone. I distanced myself more when I saw the destruction my brother, Ivan, had caused in his own daughter's life. Thalia had endured so much because of her father. He controlled her every step and even bargained her hand in marriage to gain an ally. Not uncommon in our world, but she was thirteen when he had started offering her up for allies. I was always one step ahead of Ivan to make sure Adrian and Soledad's location was hidden.

I knew all too well that Ivan Consuelo was a monster. His ability to detach from human emotions made him successful in carrying out missions and securing territories for the cartel we worked with, but it made him a horrible brother, son, and father. His need to control and exert violence was his only focus. He had an unhealthy craving to be feared amongst everyone, and he was willing to sacrifice any morals to prove himself a threat.

Growing up, we competed for our parent's affection. Everything I sought to accomplish came from a desire to honor my father's hard work and legacy. Our connections to the Houston Cartel Connect have always been professional as we laundered their money in exchange for the advancements needed to create the name we hold for ourselves. When my father and his brothers came to this country, many of his white competitors sought to destroy them with their corrupt politics and racism. The cartel protected them in exchange for a small percentage.

For Ivan, it was different. He wanted the power that came from being a member of the cartel rather than a business that benefited from them. He never cared about the legacy our father and uncles built. He wanted power and respect. When my father saw these tendencies and his thirst for power, he sent Ivan to live with his brother, Rogelio, in California.

With Ivan gone, my family could finally breathe. Especially my younger sister, Adriana, and me. We were able to live our lives more freely without him trying to control us or bully us. We started going out more, socializing, and bringing friends around. That was how I met Soledad.

Originally, she was a friend of Adriana's, but the more time she spent at the house, the more I found myself canceling plans just so I could be around her. She was unique compared to the other girls I knew. She was beautiful, and she was kind. She was a good friend to Adriana and respectful to my parents. Most of the girls I met through Saint Rita's had a false sense of entitlement that always turned me off. It wasn't long before I fell in love with her.

I was naïve to think Ivan would return and be a changed man. That I could introduce her to him and he would be happy for me. I never thought he would come back more heartless than he already was. The moment he came home and saw how much I loved Soledad, she became his next target.

Conejo walks in, drawing me out of the memory. I pour him a shot from the bottle of 1800 in front of us. He lifts his glass to me, and I return the sentiment before letting the liquor slide down my throat.

"Everything okay, compadre?"

"Ya. Just thinking about Adrian coming home." He nods. He knows the backstory. The hurt and betrayal that was involved. He was the one who helped me through the first few years, whether that meant reckless weekends in Vegas or sleepless nights in California. I wanted to drown in my sorrows. I wanted to die altogether, but he was there for me through it all. Even though I had lost Soledad, I still had to protect Adrian, so I got my shit together and did what was always expected of me.

"This is what I have so far."

Conejo hands me a manilla folder. It outlines several possible human trafficking operations within the Houston area that might have connections to Soledad. After I found out Adrian had been incarcerated, I went to visit him in the FDC. He told me about his past and his concern for Soledad. Conejo and I searched Adrian's old home and found it had been vacant for over a year. The landlord told us once Adrian got locked up, there was no money coming in to pay the rent, and Soledad was nowhere to be found. Adrian confided in me about her addiction, and I knew the root of it.

Ivan had raped her, and her overly religious parents forced her to have Adrian. A story that was not mine to share. I tried to convince her that I would say it was mine, and that we could raise Adrian together, but she could never look at me the same again. Her addiction likely stemmed from everything Ivan took from her, just as my drinking and partying were fueled by losing her. It was his final jab to let me know he was still very much in charge of our family business. He used her at his disposal, and after putting her through the hell of having his child, he left her wounds raw and open for the world to feast on.

From then on, she would find any reason to escape. He took the only thing I ever loved. He not only stole her from me, but he took her from Adrian as well. He was neglected and alone as a child and had no idea why. My family was haunted by Adrian's absence. My mother left this world wondering where he was, and my father would cry for him every time he had too much to drink. We all felt it, but never spoke of it. We would all live to know the true meaning of Soledad's name. *Loneliness.*

Chapter Three

Adrian

THREE YEARS AGO

"Kill or be killed."

That was one of the first things Conejo told me before explaining what I would need to do to prove, not only my loyalty to Los Antros, but also make my way into their inner council.

Not everyone was accepted in. My lock up order only consisted of the small crime I was set up for. I had no outside gang affiliations, and that made me useless to them. If I was going to find a way in, I would need to approach them and use the Consuelo name to my advantage just for the opportunity to join them. As soon as they learned I was Ivan Consuelo's son, they were more inclined to utilize me. I was put on a ninety-day probation period and given various small tasks, but today would be my shot at initiation.

I follow a guard with two other inmates getting initiated to a back room used for interrogations. The order was clear—work together and kill a man who had snitched on one of the inner council's kingpins on the outside. In here, there was no loyalty to a specific cartel or gang, but there were expectations to not betray your own people. On the street, snitches get stitches, but in here, death is the only accepted form of payment.

The three of us walk to the backroom. The leader of Los Antros Vidal MontaIván sits in front of a one-way mirror with his inner circle. Vidal is the son of a Colombian Kingpin. He was captured and faced a lifetime sentence. His father found him more valuable within the system than outside, so he willingly stayed.

As soon as we get to the back room, I can see why the three of us have to work together. The man we must kill stands seven-feet tall and weighs around 300 pounds of solid muscle. I also see our other disadvantage as we draw closer. The motherfucker has a knife, and we only have our fists to defend ourselves with.

As soon as we enter the room, he charges towards us. He throws me into the back wall, and I'm disoriented from the collision, but I stand up quickly. He stabs the first man in the neck. He drops immediately, and when our target bends down to remove the knife from the lifeless body, I take the opportunity to choke him from behind. My partner begins to punch him as I squeeze harder, waiting for the life to drain out of him, but the son of a bitch is strong. He struggles to get me off his back, and, in the process, he drops the knife. He frees himself from me, throwing me back into the concrete wall as he falls to the ground, coughing and trying to catch his breath.

"Stab him," I yell to my partner, but he's stalling. We have no time to waste, and I can't trust someone who needs to stop and check-in with their conscience. Kill or Be Killed. The words repeat themselves over and over in my head. I didn't come this far to only get this far. I lunge forward and reach for the knife just in time to slit our target's throat. But I'm not done yet.

I turn to the last man, who is still in shock, staring at the two bodies on the floor and the blood surrounding us. I don't think twice before I begin to stab him repeatedly. Blood splatters onto me and I watch as his life drains from him. I don't stop until the guards walk in to grab me. Before they drag me to solitary confinement, Vidal stops me in the hall.

"Bienvenido, Adriano."

He sent welcoming gifts to me in solitary confinement, and I received one of many care packages that first day.

From then on, I did what I had to do to survive. Every mission or task Vidal threw at me, I completed. I started as a category one and within the first year, I was voted in as a category three member. I grew to understand the power of authority and just how far respect would get me. I used that respect to bring Efren into Los Antros, and together, we became invincible.

"Adriano, how will you serve me beyond these walls?"

Vidal sits across from me in a similar orange suit. I told him about my upcoming parole meeting that Patricio set up for me.

"Wherever you want to put me, Jefe," I say and he nods. Vidal has no use for me outside these walls. He runs most of his operations through Miami, but I knew he was eager to move in through the West Coast.

"I want to expand the few operations I have in Texas. My nephew, Ricky, will be moving there and will work to obtain a real estate license we will need to advance our outside operations. In the meantime, he answers to the Houston Cartel Connect, and I will sanction any members you request coming in." He stands to walk out, and I know this means goodbye for now.

The years I spent here were coming to an end. I am not the same person who walked into this prison. The blood on my hands has changed me. I'm not sure if society is ready for me. My enemies are still out there, and the person I've had to become to survive all these years is the last person you want as an enemy.

Chapter Four

Mireya

I was the first to show up at the bar on Thursday. It was a weekly tradition. Thalia, Alma, and I met up for drinks every Thursday in the hotel's bar. Alma and I shared an apartment in downtown Houston, but I barely saw her with school and work. We met during my first year of college, when Alma thought she was going to be a preschool teacher but couldn't handle the amount of boogers she had to clean. She decided to take some time off of school to figure it out, and now works as a housekeeper full time for Calavera Hotels.

Thalia was best described as a Mexican Goth Barbie. A name Alma gave her after the first time they met. Where Alma was sunshine and rainbows, Thalia was a modern day Wednesday Addams in heels with cartel ties. She held the title of Chief Financial Officer, but over the years,

Alma and I noticed she held a much higher position as Patricio's protégé. I knew her decision to keep that part of her life private was also how she protected us.

She was the one who introduced me to Dr. Aguilar. He and I quickly connected, and it wasn't too long before he would call me to assist him. He or Thalia would call me to scenes where men were shot down, half dead or injured. Before I knew it, I became his permanent assistant, and somehow, my hours and pay miraculously increased at the hotel. I did my best not to ask too many questions or get myself too involved. I needed the extra money to pay for school and pay off the credit card debt I had acquired trying to survive.

I was unsure how Adrian might fit into all of this. I knew he had always been a hard worker. I look down at the bracelet he had given me when we were younger. He worked his ass off that summer mowing lawns just so he could give it to me on my birthday. I was afraid to think of what would happen when he saw me again.

I order a round of shots and top shelf margaritas. Mango flavor for me, blackberry for Thalia, and watermelon for Alma.

"Damn bitch, you starting early?" Alma says as she squeezes into the booth I reserved for the three of us. She is still in her maid uniform, her curly brown hair pulled up in a bun. She looks exhausted, but still offers me a smile. She has natural beauty with her flawless skin. It makes sense, since she has an hour-long bedtime routine and enough discipline to avoid dairy.

We order our usual appetizers and wait for Thalia. Alma pulls out bottles of Tajin and Chamoy that she carries in her purse and preps our drinks. We always tell her she would make a good bartender, but she says the crowd is too intimidating. She loves her job as a maid because she can listen to her fairy smut books and be in her own world while cleaning and reorganizing rooms. Enrique adores her because she pays so much attention to detail.

Thalia walks in finally, and she is ready to make a statement, as always. She is wearing black dress pants with a matching black turtleneck tank top and Louboutin heels. Her arms are toned and covered in tattoos. Black matte lipstick, her signature touch.

"Hey, putas!" she says and makes her way to the table. "You have no fucking idea how much I need this."

She slouches into the booth and grabs her drink. We all clink glasses and start the night. This was the only time we were guaranteed a bit of relief from work, and life. We would often sit in this corner booth, venting our weekly struggles, while ending the night making fools of ourselves as we sang drunk karaoke. There was not one Vicente

Fernandez song that was not victimized by us by the end of the night.

We have been sitting in the corner booth for a few hours when Olivia Consuelo joins us. She runs the restaurant and shares a penthouse upstairs with Thalia and her two kids, Lucia and Luca. Even though she is Thalia's aunt, they act more like sisters, only a few years separating them in age. We order our third round of shots as Alma fills us in on all the chisme going on with the maids, which was better than any novela, since Alma is a natural at acting and doing impressions. Olivia declines the shot we offer her and sneaks out to put the kids to bed.

Thalia lets us in on her newest endeavors of her dating life. Last week being another failed Tinder match with a guy, who thought it would be funny to do an Austin Powers impression during foreplay. Alma spits out her drink as Thalia mocks the guy, lowering her voice to say, "How does it feel, baby," after she requested he go lower.

Usually I would just listen to them both vent. Really my life wasn't ever exciting enough to talk about. Thalia had enough sex for both Alma and I. I hadn't gone on a date in years. Thalia had bought me a vibrator when I told her I hadn't had sex since Bryan, and Alma had tried to set me up on double dates. One time, she even tried setting me up with a woman from her book club, just because all her other attempts with men failed.

The truth is, I just don't feel interested in it much anymore. Sometimes on my days off, I feel too tired to even do anything but lie in bed. And I only get over these depressive states by throwing myself into work. I think Dr. Aguilar sees this and often calls me to help him just to keep me busy.

I could easily marry Dr. Aguilar, since he is the only man I feel comfortable even being alone around since breaking up with Bryan. I even asked Thalia if he had a girlfriend once, and she busted up laughing, saying he was gayer than Walter Mercado riding a rainbow unicorn while touring with Elton John. Just my luck.

I don't want to tell the girls about how fucked up I've been this week since finding out about Bryan and Adrian in the same day. I trust them both not to judge me, but there is still an insecure part of me that is convinced our friendship isn't real. I have this fear that if they saw the real me–the needy, weak part of me–that they would dip out like everyone else in my life. But liquid courage be damned, I decide to bring it up.

"I think the universe hates me," I say, interrupting Alma trying to convince Thalia to read one of her books. They both look over at me. I clear my throat. "Monday, I had to talk to Bryan and Diana's wedding planner. Their engagement party is going to be here." I hold up the shot Olivia left and take it down while Alma gasps.

"Are you serious?"

They both know about my fucked-up relationship with Bryan. After all my fake friends had abandoned me at Saint Rita's, I was all alone. It wasn't until my senior year, when Thalia moved back from California, that she befriended me and helped me to heal with all her witchy self-love rituals. I would always be grateful to her for that. But I never mentioned Adrian during all that. I honestly never thought we'd cross paths again.

"It gets worse." I turn to face Thalia.

"Your cousin, Adrian, who is also my ex-boyfriend, is coming out of prison and moving into the vacant penthouse."

Thalia's eyes widen before she lets out a drunk laugh.

"Adrian is not my cousin." She's still laughing, apparently already intoxicated, as she lets out the next part. "He's my half-brother."

Alma gasps again. I swear her dramatic effects put the entire cast of La Rosa de Guadalupe to shame.

"Wait. Shut up! You have a half-brother and never told us about him?" She points at Thalia and then to me. "And you dated him?"

She crosses herself like a nun and finishes her margarita.

I am still silent as I try to understand. Thalia and Adrian are brother and sister?

"I know your cousins are hot as hell, so I can only imagine what your brother looks like," Alma says, and I, for some reason, shoot her a dirty look.

"Sorry. So, who is older?" I ask Thalia, trying to piece this part of Adrian's life together. He never told me about any of this. "I think I'm like 6 months older," Thalia says.

"So, you're basically like Irish twins," Alma says.

"Um, no. And seriously, this conversation is a buzzkill. Can we stop talking about him? I'm sorry, Mireya. Sober me will help you through all this, I swear, but I prefer not to think of my father and his thousands of estranged children right now. Childhood trauma and whatnot."

I feel bad for even bringing it up. My brain goes to creating fake scenarios where both girls unfriend me, and I wash the toxic thoughts down with the remainder of my margarita. I'm grateful when Alma leads us to the karaoke machine. We order more drinks before we ruin everyone's night with our version of "Por Tu Maldito Amor".

Chapter Five

Adrian

I'm finally fucking free. I walk out to see Patricio standing in front of his Rolls Royce Phantom. He wears a designer suit with his hair slicked back, facial hair trimmed, and rings covering his tattooed knuckles. I flick the cigarette I had been smoking and stand, grabbing ahold of what little I have to leave with. In the six years I stayed locked up, I never once imagined this was how I would leave. In a Rolls Royce with my estranged uncle who makes seven figures running a hotel and laundering money for the cartel.

Three years ago, when he came looking for me, I had no idea what I would be getting myself into. My mother had gone into one of her drug binges after I was sentenced, so I hadn't seen or heard from her, and I had been worried she was finally losing the battle to her addiction. The longer she went without visiting me, the more anxious I became that I would receive a call about her death.

A part of me had hoped it would be her on the other end of the glass when they told me I had a visitor that day. I had created a coping mechanism as a kid, when I first noticed my mom was an addict. Instead of worrying about what she was doing, I would imagine her safe, checking herself into rehab. After a while, I stopped lying to myself and found other ways to cope. I had to take care of myself and keep a roof over our heads.

When I got up to the window, I had looked up to see a face I didn't recognize at the time.

I pick up the phone.

"Adriano, my name is Patricio Consuelo. I am your biological uncle, and I have been looking for you. There is a long history, but if you are willing to trust me, I think I have a way to get you out of here."

A part of me had wanted to hang up on the son of a bitch. The brokenness in me wanted to tell him and his entire family to fuck off. Everyone in Houston knew about Calavera Hotels and the family was notorious for the wealth they had accumulated over the years. I was confused. My mother had told me she didn't know who my father was, and that's why I had her maiden name as my last name. None of it made any sense.

"Why isn't my father here?" I ask.

Patricio's eyes are blank. He stares back at me pausing for a moment.

"In time, I will tell you everything you want to know. My brother was not a good man, and everything your mother and you suffered was a direct attack towards me. It's not my story to tell, and when we find your mother, I will give her the opportunity to tell you. She deserves that."

I respected him for telling me what he could. Over the course of my remaining time at FDC, I found it easy to confide in Patricio. He would pass what he could to me through Izeiah, one of the guards, who he had strategically placed on the inside. I had spoken with him about Bryan and asked him to find out all the information regarding my case, so when I got out, I could get my revenge.

"Adriano," Patricio says with a nod as he opens the back door for me, and my focus comes back to the present.

I nod back, then get in the back seat. I hope he wasn't expecting a hug or some sentiment, as our relationship was always through a piece of glass. I just spent six years with nothing but men, and the last thing I want is a hug. Thankfully, he sticks out his hand, and I return the gesture to greet him.

Once we are in the car, he instructs his driver to take us to the hotel, where he has set me up in one of the vacant penthouses.

"I have all your parole documents set to your new home address at the hotel, and I have listed your occupation as maintenance."

I laugh at the word. *Maintenance.* This is his subtle way of letting me know I'll be Conejo's right hand bitch, but whatever has to be done to convince my parole officers I am blending into society.

"I have something else for you," he says and pulls out two manilla envelopes and hands them to me.

"What's this?"

"The first one is several properties we'll need to strategically take down to see if your mother is a part of their human trafficking ring. The second is Bryan's alibi from the night he set you up."

Curious, I open the first folder. A bunch of addresses and photos of the people who own the homes. I'll go over them more tomorrow. I open the second folder and stop when I see her. *Mireya Torres.* I'm not surprised she was his alibi. I always suspected it to be her, but a part of me thought she would never do that to me. Another coping mechanism, I guess. I am surprised to see her after all this time. The pictures are from a distance, but I notice her immediately. Her body has matured with time. She's standing with a phone in her hand as she bends down to scribble on to a notepad. The angle forcing her shirt up a little and her ass popped out. Other pictures show her in scrubs, coming out of the hospital. I had read in the file that she was in nursing school. She spends the mornings at school and then spends her evenings working the front desk at the hotel. A few pictures are from hotel events, one of her in a short black spaghetti- strap dress, laughing with her friends. Her smooth legs on display. Something in me wants to beat the shit out of whoever took these pictures of her, but I have to remind myself she is not anything to me. She is my enemy.

I sit there examining the photos a little bit longer. I like the ones of her working. She still wears her hair long, straightened down to the middle of her back and her makeup is simple. She looks professional in her all-black uniform, but the Cortez shoes, the big hoops, and lined lips still scream of the hood we grew up in.

She had always been mine. The day I saw her walking home from school and some kids were picking on her, I beat all their asses. She was an escape from all the shit I had going on in my house. We never got past making out and dry humping in her bedroom while her parents were gone. Even if our love was young and innocent, it felt real to me at that time. I have no idea who the girl in these pictures is anymore.

"Do you know her?" Patricio asks, taking in my intense observation.

"She's my ex-girlfriend," I say as I put the pictures back and look out the window.

"She works for us at the hotel. She's a good worker and Thalia's best friend. I like her, but I won't make excuses for her. I won't deny you your revenge. The choice is yours about what you want to do with her. Her address, school, acquaintances, and schedule are all in the envelope."

I wasn't sure how or when, but the decision was easy. The more I think about her and Bryan, the more I want to wreak havoc on her perfect little life. *I want to punish her.*

Chapter Six

Adrian

After picking me up, Patricio helped me to get some clothes and other necessities I needed. He asked what meal I had craved the most while locked up and laughed when I told him I wanted him to take me to the greasiest taco truck he could find.

By the time we make our way to the hotel, it is late, and there is little to no staff working. The hotel is bigger than I had imagined. There are three large buildings, each with thirteen floors that surround several outdoor pools. The entire hotel is painted in matte black, with accents of skulls and goth-inspired décor. I am tired, but Patricio insists on giving me a tour. There is a fine dining restaurant, a bar, event rooms, and past the front desk are stairs that lead to several offices.

We make our way up to the penthouse I'll be staying in.

"It was already furnished, but you are more than welcome to make any changes," he says as he opens the door. *Anything's better than prison.*

It's bigger than any house or apartment I lived in growing up. We moved around a lot, depending on what we could afford and how many bridges my mom had burnt. There are three bedrooms, a large living room, kitchen, and a patio with a pool overlooking the city lights. Patricio had been asking me what things I would need when I got out. His questions ranged from my daily routine to the style of clothes I liked. I'm impressed when I see the middle room set up with free weights and exercise equipment. Los Antros taught me a lot about discipline. Those of us who had it would wake up early every day to train and keep our minds focused.

"Thalia helped with the clothes."

I follow him to the back bedroom closet that's filled with basic solid color tees, pro clubs, Ben Davis hoodies, and Dickies pants. Several pairs of white tennis shoes and... *cowboy boots?*

"Those were a gift from Conejo." Patricio laughs at my facial expression. "As were these." He opens the doors on a black cabinet, and inside, it is filled with guns, ropes, and other weapons fit for a sicario.

"Tomorrow, we will go to the training compound so

you can meet the guys you will be working with. It's important you remember that when we are working, I'm not your tio; I am your boss, and I will have expectations of you. I can't let the other men see you being favored."

"Don't worry about me. I know how to gain respect." I only spent the last three years gaining the respect of one of the most notorious prison gangs in Houston. I could hold my own. Patricio nods in agreement.

"Get some rest. I'll see you in the morning."

I take a long, hot shower before heading to bed. It's simple things like this that I missed. Showering without a time limit, eating something other than ramen, and walking around naked. I make some sopa de fideo before I head to the room to sleep. I take the manilla envelopes with me and take out the pictures of Mireya.

I had many conjugal visits, thanks to the courtesy of Vidal, but I don't remember my dick being as hard as it is right now, just looking at her pictures. I can only imagine how her pouty lips would feel wrapped around my dick. How her hair would feel wrapped in my fists. I developed a deranged taste for sex since I had been locked up. Some of the women who came to visit would have particular needs or kinks they wanted fulfilled, and I learned quickly to explore my own kinks.

I grab a cigarette from the nightstand. I would torment

myself a bit before I fall asleep. Maybe I would jack off and cum all over these photos.

I thought for sure I would be able to sleep all day, but sleeping in was 10AM for me, and then I was up, and my body needed its regular routine. I worked out for an hour, ate breakfast, and then showered before I got ready and headed downstairs.

I'm headed to meet Patricio when I see a familiar face checking in an older couple and handing them their key. She doesn't notice me at first, but the moment she does, her cheeks flush. I look straight at her. She is wearing the same uniform from the pictures. A black polo t-shirt with Calavera Hotels embroidered in red with marigolds and roses beneath it.

Before I can decide on what to say to her, I see a shadow descending the stairs. The figure steps out, and I recognize the similar features, the same nose, the same eyes with long lashes, high cheekbones, and full lips, but hers are painted black.

Thalia Consuelo.

My half-sister.

I walk past both of them to the staircase. I'm too tired

to deal with an emotional family reunion. Thalia wrote to me a few times while I was away. It was in her letters that I found out more about the waste of space that was our biological father. She poured her heart out in those letters, telling me how Ivan had ruined her life. Even though he didn't abandon her and her mom, he also did not stop her mom's abduction and death when Thalia was ten years old. I know Thalia would have almost preferred he had abandoned them over the pain of knowing him and what he was capable of.

I had to remind myself the coward was dead, and I didn't need a reminder more than myself that he ever existed. I know Thalia is not to be blamed, but it is still a sharp reminder of the broken parts of my mother. The broken parts of me.

Once I make it up the stairs, I turn into Patricio's office. He is sitting at his desk when he looks up to see me standing in the doorway. We have company, it appears, and while I recognize Conejo, I am not familiar with the older man in a cowboy hat sitting on the couch. His smile lights up when I enter the room.

Conejo stands to shake my hand. "Como estas, cabrón? Did you get my gifts?" he says, and I nod, laughing as I take his hand.

"I did. I'll be dead before I wear those ugly things."

"Everything okay in the penthouse?" Patricio asks.

"Todo bien." I say, letting him know everything is okay, but my eyes observe the stranger.

"I wanted you to meet your grandfather." He motions towards the old man, who stands with his hand out. When I give my hand, he holds it as he smiles at me. For a second, it's as if something like sadness washes over him. We stand observing one another. He wears a flannel and some jeans with his boots and a cowboy hat on his head.

"I wanted to see you for myself. You held yourself well when you were locked up, but I want to make sure this life is something you choose, Adrian."

"I don't think I have a choice when it comes to survival, but if you're questioning my loyalty, then I can assure you I've earned my place."

Conejo nods in agreement as my grandfather continues to take me in, that sadness still lingering.

"What's the plan to find my mom?" I ask Patricio to avoid the looks of Vicente Consuelo. So much for avoiding emotional baggage today.

"Today, you'll want to go to the compound and get to know the men you'll be working with. Ricky got here last week and has been training with the men. We'll start with the first house, but we'll need to send in spies. Pa, did you get the cellphone I told you to get for Adrian?" He looks at Vicente.

"I don't know nothing about that shit. I had Thalia go get it."

A knock comes at the door and Conejo walks to open it.

Thalia stands outside, arms crossed and a phone box in her hand.

"Abuelo, are you trading me in for a new favorite grandchild?" She looks at me and smiles softly. Don Vicente laughs as she makes her way to hug him. She hands me a box with an iPhone inside.

"It's activated, but it's not set up yet. Let me know if you need help." Her words are cold and sharp as she hands me the phone.

"Ven, Mija, grab the good bottle of tequila. We have something good to celebrate."

She grabs the bottle and pours out five shots.

"To family," Patricio says, and with that, we all drink.

A few shots and an hour-long story from Don Vicente on the history of Calavera Hotels, and I make my way back down to the lobby.

"Adrian," I barely hear her whisper behind me. I turn to see Mireya just inches from me. I take in her presence. She smells like vanilla, and I want to lean in to take in more of it. I look right at her. She has a fearful look in her eyes, like I'm a ghost she's seeing for the first time. Her lips are slightly parted, and my damn cock still wonders what it would be like to slide in between them. My brain, however, is still hellbent on destruction, so I decide then and there to be petty.

"I'm sorry... do I know you?"

Chapter Seven

Mireya

I'm sitting in the break room at the hotel reading over my study guide before my shift starts. I use my front teeth to scrape off the pink gel polish on my fingernails. A nervous habit I adopted in elementary school. I'd scrape off the polish and then spit out the gel residue. Over and over again, until I removed all the polish from every fingernail. It was weird. I know. The habit was only one step above eating Tide pods, but I couldn't stop now. Not with the tests I had coming up, and Adrian's presence here at the hotel as a constant distraction. The stress is accumulating.

"I'm sorry... do I know you?"

It's been three days since Adrian returned, and he is still acting like I'm some stranger. Thalia has been on edge since his return. At least I'm not the only one he's ignoring. Thalia has used her frustration as an excuse to go into

Enrique's office and start a fight with her uncle. I listen as she walks in and demands to know why the hotel is still hosting Bryan and Diana's engagement party. That only pisses Enrique off. The two of them are always in some type of pissing contest. I listen to the insults they throw at each other, despite being two floors down.

Anytime Thalia and Enrique bump heads, the rest of the front desk staff have to deal with the tension they create. I had already known this week would be hell. I am in my head about Adrian not recognizing me. I had barely slept the first night, trying to make sense of it. I hadn't changed that much. He had seen me around after our breakup. Coincidently, he even walked into a party where I was sitting on Bryan's lap. He looked at us and shook his head before leaving.

I settle on the idea that he got hit in the head while he was in prison. I knew from the countless times Thalia made me watch Blood In Blood Out that there were daily fights in prison. It's possible he had suffered a concussion, and it messed with his memory. That seems better than having to admit that I had over-romanticized our short-lived relationship. It was a fling. He probably had a lot of flings. Either way, I need to let it go. It could work to my benefit if he had actually forgotten me because that would mean he's unaware that I was Bryan's alibi.

I clock into work and head to the front desk. It's quiet tonight, but most Monday nights are. I have two fingernails still left with polish on them. I am already anticipating another awkward run in with Adrian. Yesterday, I ran into him coming down the stairs. His body was rock solid, and he just looked at me as if he could see through me before walking around me. Later, he called me Mariah, and I didn't even correct him despite it being my biggest pet peeve with customers.

"Stop picking at your polish." I turn to see Thalia coming down the stairs. "If Enrique sees you, he'll crucify you, and then I'll have to kill him for reals."

I drop my hand, but she notices the concern on my face.

"What's wrong? Is it Bryan, because I swear to God..."

"No. It's okay," I say more to myself than her. "I am honestly over it. I can't avoid him forever, so if he shows up, I just need to confront this head on. It's been six years, and I need to just get over it." If Adrian can forget me in six years, then surely I can forget Bryan.

"It was an abusive relationship. Don't let anyone make you feel like you should *just get over it*. You decide when and how you heal. Just stop eating your nail polish, okay?" She offers a genuine smile and we both laugh. She takes another look at me and sucks in a deep breath, her eyes double checking mine to make sure I'm really okay.

Thalia is the only person I feel comfortable enough to confess all the things that Bryan had done to humiliate me. Fucking me in front of his friends while they video recorded it, offering his friends blow jobs and asking me to pay off his drug debts with my body. I willingly did those things, but I always felt dirty afterwards. I was always afraid if I said no, that he would break things off with me.

It wasn't until he broke up with me that I started to recognize how manipulative the entire situation was.

The first night I told her about everything he would have me do, she was pissed. Then her anger turned to sadness, and she hugged me while we both cried. One of the first and only times both of us had cried like that. One of the only times I let myself cry, despite my mother's voice lingering in my head. *You look ugly when you cry.*

Thalia told me that night that she understood what it felt like to have a man destroy you. I knew she meant her father. She never talked about that part of her life, but I knew there was a lot she had suffered at his hands. I never pushed her to talk about it. I let her be a closed book when it came to her emotions. Not all of us can feel and express ourselves the way Alma does.

"If they show up unannounced, just let me know. I don't care what Enrique says. I will feed him his own balls for dinner."

"Feeding who balls?" I hear the deep voice and glance over my shoulder to see Adrian. His big brown eyes meet mine, and I quickly turn my head back to my desk. He towers over my five-foot frame from behind, and I can feel the warmth of him radiating outwards. I don't have to look to know he's scowling at me. It is his common facial expression whenever I am in his vicinity.

Thalia turns to stand in front of the desk, facing both of us. Her eyes narrow as she stares at him. While I know she wants a relationship with her brother, I also know she is the last person to beg for anything. I can already see the fury in her eyes as she looks him over. She is still in fight mode.

"He speaks! Frankenstein's monster speaks and blesses us with his presence," she says, as she exaggerates her arms opening to the fake crowd.

Adrian reaches over me and grabs the maintenance clipboard in front of me. It's quick, but something builds inside me as his body heat envelops me. He smells like Tres Flores Pomade—a mix of jasmine and chrysanthemum. I inhale him, remembering that familiar scent. He barely skims my ass, and I feel tingles run through my body. My cheeks flush, and I refuse to turn back toward him.

"I'm not Enrique. I refuse to be insulted by some béli-cona who looks like she fucks in graveyards for fun." His insult gets his desired effect. I watch as the rage crashes over Thalia. Bélicona was Enrique's favorite name for her when they were arguing. It made sense, since she was something of a narco princess who divulged in that lifestyle. She refused to be too relatable to a singular stereotype, though. She was chic, she was goth, and she was bélica.

She was fine referring to herself as that, but Enrique called her that out of spite. The same way my mother would call me 'princess' to mock me. Adrian calling her that clearly struck a nerve.

"Aww. How nice of you to notice my weekday hobbies." She has that crazy look in her eyes. He walks away, and she grabs me and pulls me with her to follow him.

Adrian ignores her as he reaches into the fridge to grab a sandwich. Don Mario is in there eating his lunch, and Adrian sits in the chair next to him. I try not to stare at Adrian too long, but there's something about the way he has matured since I saw him last. His body is fuller and muscular. My eyes nervously scan him from head to toe before I look away.

I memorize his features in the short glimpse. His brown eyes and long lashes, the mole under his left eyebrow, the tattoos scattered across his neck and arms. He wears an all-white shirt, a gold chain, and blue Dickies pants. He keeps his hair as I remember, cut short and faded on the sides. He continues to eat his food, starting a conversation with Don Mario. I can see the mischief on Thalia's face. She pulls me to sit next to her at the table across from Adrian.

"Mireya, how incredibly rude of me. I almost forgot to introduce you two. This is my half brother, Adriano. Adriano, this is my best friend, Mireya."

He keeps on his façade as he smiles at me and extends his hand.

"Nice to meet you." Like a complete idiot, I take his hand and shake it. The warmth of my hand in his brings back the tingles from earlier. I pull my hand back quickly and look away.

"You know Mireya grew up in the same neighborhood as you?" she says accusatorily, and I feel humiliated for her and me. What the hell is she doing? He wipes the mayo from the side of his lip, and I watch like it's the first time I'd seen porn. He licks his lip, and the act is so seductive I am convinced this is now a kink of mine.

Note-to self: research sandwich eating kink later.

When he speaks, his voice is low and husky.

"I don't remember seeing her, but then again, I was in prison for six years." He stares straight at me. Fire blazes in his eyes, and the tension is so thick you could cut it with a knife. Don Mario breaks the silence when he opens a beer. Enrique has told him several times he can't drink on the job, but he doesn't care. We turn to look at him and listen to the weird noises he makes as he chugs the beer down.

"Anyone want a cookie?" he says and pulls out a box of cookies dusted in powdered sugar. He offers one to Adrian first, who takes a bite. He pushes the box towards Thalia and me, and we each take one. Then, in a matter of seconds, Adrian leans forward and smacks the cookie out of my hand. Thalia jumps up, ready to fight him, but he just walks past us and throws away his trash before exiting the break room. But not before he turns around and looks right at me.

"They have orange zest in them."

"Orange zest? What the fuck is he talking about?" Thalia shouts.

"I'm allergic to oranges," I whisper. Even Thalia forgot this, despite me telling her about it a thousand times. *So, he does remember me.*

Chapter Eight

Adrian

I'm sitting in the passenger seat of a black van with Osiel and Ricky as we drive through, collecting money from different banks and organizations that operate under the guise of the cartel. I'm still trying to figure out my phone when I see an incoming call from the FDC. I had been waiting for Efren to call me back so I could check in with him.

"Hello?"

"Hey, big homie. I haven't been able to call. They're trying to move me to a detention center." I knew Efren was considered illegal, despite spending his whole life here. He could have applied for his citizenship at eighteen, but we were only seventeen when we were tried as adults. His foster parents couldn't legally adopt him without admitting to their own crimes.

"I'll talk to Patricio. Don't worry about it."

"I'm thinking of just going back. There's some work Vidal wants me to do and, honestly, I think it's time I meet my parents." I go silent, and he knows what I won't say. I need him here with me. The guys I work with are reliable, but I don't trust anyone the way I trust Efren. We have been raising ourselves for years, and we would take a bullet for each other if we had to.

"Did you give her the letter?" he asks, and I already know who. I didn't ask a lot of questions, but Efren wanted me to deliver a letter to Alma Guiterez, his brother's ex-girlfriend.

"Yeah, your sources were right. She works at the hotel as a maid. I gave it to her this morning."

"Thanks. I don't want to interfere with her life, but I owe it to my brother to make sure she's alright." I don't push the subject, and he doesn't have to explain shit to me. I never explained my whole newfound rich family or the cartel shit I dragged him into with me.

The fifteen minutes run out and I return my focus to work. The three of us are on our way to Conejo's ranch.

"Look at all these billetes!" Ricky says, and I look back to see we've filled the entire back of the van with bags of money. We get to the front gates of Conejo's ranch. He has guards spread out all over the property. We make it up a large hill to see a large green house. When we pass by it, I see a woman around my age watering flowers. She has long blonde hair and waves as we pass by.

Ricky whistles low from the back seat as Osiel drives on to the back of the property where the warehouse sits.

"How does someone as ugly as Conejo make a fine ass daughter like that?"

"Nah, fool. I'm not into orgies," Osiel says, and we look at him, confused.

"I've known her since I was a toddler. I'm telling you, homegirl has like seven different personalities in one. Could you imagine trying to have sex with all of them?"

I shake my head and Ricky lets out a laugh.

"No mames!" Ricky says in disbelief. Osiel is always joking about something. We drive a few more miles until we reach the warehouse. Several trucks are parked out front, ready to take their loads. We divide the money between the different dealers before splitting our cut of it. It's a promotion for me not having to directly touch drugs or kill someone for pay. A perk of being a Consuelo, I presume. I'm about to get back in the van when Conejo pulls me aside.

"Did you see my daughter, Genesis, out front?"

"Ya. I mean, we all saw her. She was watering flowers," I say, assuming he wanted us to check on her.

"What did you think?" *Shit.* I already know where this conversation is going. Conejo is old school. He believes in arranged marriages, and because he trusts me, he wants to give her to me. Flattering. But she's not my type. I barely noticed her when we passed by. My thoughts are still stuck on a certain brunette with big brown eyes and that intoxicating smell of vanilla. The feel of her ass molding into me when I reached over her the other day.

"I'm not trying to settle down just yet," I say, and he nods.

"She's a good girl. She's obedient, knows how to cook, cleans, and doesn't talk back. When you're ready to settle down, you let me know, and she's yours, vato." He says it like she's one of his animals he's trying to auction off. Like those qualities would be a selling point. To me, it just sounds safe and boring as hell. Now I just felt bad for the girl.

It's late when we get back to the hotel. Osiel and Ricky convince me to join them for a few drinks in the hotel bar before I head up. When I walk in, I see Mireya and Alma in a corner booth. My eyes roam over Mireya. Her hair is up in a ponytail, gold hoops dangle from her ears. She's still in her work pants, but she's removed the polo top, and in its place is a thin, black spaghetti-strap tank top. Her large boobs on full display. My mouth waters like I've been stranded for days in the desert. Alma catches me staring and shoots me a dirty look.

"That one has veneno for blood," Ricky says, and I look to see Thalia walking in to join them. I would bet the 10K I made today to back Ricky's claim. She most definitely has poison or some other toxin in her blood. I watch as he stares her up and down. *Gross.* I look and see Osiel is a bit more respectful and adverts his eyes back to the bar. He's just here for a good time. The cartel funds his father's construction business. A business that he would be taking over soon, since his dad played his cards right. I heard stories about his father while I was in prison. Someone crossed him and he cemented their body into one of his construction sites. They would be the ideal partners going forward, when Vidal was ready to expand his operations in the real estate market.

I listen to the conversation between Osiel and the bartender, but my eyes never leave Mireya. Osiel must have noticed me staring when he comes up beside me. He hands me a Modelo and uses the end of his beer bottle to point it towards Mireya. "You know her?"

"I used to," I say before I take a swig of my beer.

"Before you went to prison or what?"

"We grew up in the same hood. I was just wondering what the last six years looked like for her." He fiddles with his phone before looking up at me.

"Well, according to Instagram, not much." He leans in to show me something on his phone. I look quickly at his screen. I don't want to seem too desperate, but Osiel has already picked up on my curiosity.

"Oh, we are making you an account, homie. How else you going to get laid in 2024?"

Within an hour, he makes me a profile with a picture and follows himself and some porn stars. He shows me how easy it was to find her, since he and Alma were friends. She has a ton of tagged pictures of them out together. Then he gives Ricky and I a brief course on IG stalking.

"Rule #1: Don't like anything. It will notify her you liked it, and she'll know you were creepin. Rule #2: Never watch her stories or lives. She can see who watches the stories. And bet your ass she will block you. Or worse, she'll put you on blast and tag you. Eliminating any chance you may have had with one of her homegirls."

He is obviously talking from experience. The guy has a PhD in failed relationships and an understudy in internet stalking. I'm not sure what was creepier—the fact he knew all this or the way Ricky is taking in all the info and writing notes on his phone. I zone out when he starts on his Tinder lesson.

I don't have time to figure out a dating app nor am I interested. I just need to figure out what Mireya has been up to the last six years. It's like an itch I need to scratch, and I convince myself it is fueled by my need for revenge. Surely, it has nothing to do with the way I feel every time I look at her. This longing need to see what she hides under the thin material of her tank top. The smell of her arousal. The taste of her orgasm. Fuck. I just need to look at her page once. Scratch the itch and continue on like we never knew each other. A plan I already screwed up after tasting the orange in Don Mario's cookies and warning her.

Time flies when you're stalking your ex-girlfriend. The bartender calls out for last call and I move to pay our tab. While Osiel was crafting a horrific Tinder bio for Ricky, I spent most the night looking up the last six years of Mireya's life. You'd think she was the one who was in prison, as there were very few pictures of her. Most of the ones I found were tagged on Thalia and Alma's Insta-grams. She never posted a picture of her by herself. Most of her posts are pictures of her, Thalia, and Alma. There are a ton of nurse memes, pictures of food, and a ton of pictures of a fat cat. *A cat lady.* I hated cats. But it's better than seeing pictures of her and Bryan. There is absolutely no sign of Bryan. No sign of any guy. No sign of her mom, who probably still hates me. Her highlights, which Osiel said were safe to stalk, are mostly a recap of their Thursday nights and family events with the Consuelos. She's spent the last 6 years more involved with my biological family than I have been.

I leave the bar and head to the elevator, where a very drunk Thalia and Mireya are trying to help an unconscious Alma get in. They finally get her in, and before the doors can close, I squeeze myself through. Alma's leaning against the elevator wall as she passes out. Mireya holds her up and Thalia is laughing on the floor. Mireya sighs in frustration. She's the soberest of the three of them. She avoids eye contact with me, as usual. Anytime I am around, she looks at anything but me. It's like she is afraid of what would happen if she looks directly at me. Good. She should be afraid of me. *She is my enemy.*

She bites down on her bottom lip and I press the button up to the thirteenth floor. I'm fighting my carnal urge to pick her up and drag her to my room when the elevator doors open. I watch as Mireya tries to get both Thalia and Alma out, but it's a bit of a struggle.

I move to Thalia's side, and she looks up at me, her eyes glazed over. "Frankenstein," she says, then begins laughing hysterically again. I reach down and pick her up, motioning to Mireya to show me the way.

"Come on, loca. Let's get you home," I say as she continues laughing like a madwoman. If her head starts spinning around, I will drop her ass so fast. I was down to kill anyone who crossed me, but what I was not willing to do was fight a demon possessed bitch. Mireya guides me to Thalia's penthouse. Thalia lives with Olivia, my biological aunt, and her twin children.

Olivia opens the door and she looks tired. We obviously woke her up. She looks down at Thalia and sighs.

"Let me guess. Top Shelf Thursday?" she says, as Thalia starts to mumble a refute. She looks upset as she looks down on Thalia, but when her eyes meet mine, she gives me a warm smile. Olivia motions to enter and leads me to the back bedroom. "Shhh," she whispers. "The kids are sleeping."

Their penthouse is much bigger than the one I'm staying in. There's a large kitchen and a dining room off to the side. The walls are covered with pictures of Thalia, Olivia, and the two children.

"That's Lucia and Luca. The twins," Mireya says from behind me. She smiles softly and I nod. She passes me, and I follow her to a back room. The room is full of gothic décor. Framed horror movie posters line the walls. All the movies from the late 70s, early 80s. The Omen, Carrie, and

The Awakening.

"Thank you," Olivia says, and I drop Thalia on the bed, watching her fall to the mattress hard. She reaches for her head and groans. Olivia's eyes widen as she stifles a laugh. As a kid, I always felt alone and wanted a sibling. Now that I had Wednesday Addams as a sister, I wasn't too thrilled. Thalia starts laughing again, and Olivia rolls her eyes and slams the door behind us. She leads us into the kitchen and goes to the back room to get Alma a blanket.

"They all love you, and I know you are all still trying to get to know one another, but they are good people." I turn to look at Mireya, into her big brown eyes. Something about the way she looks at me brings me back to a time when I thought we'd be together forever. Memories of her arms wrapped around me, the letters she would write me, our late night phone conversations. I never once let those memories disturb me while I was locked up. I never thought of her, and now that she has appeared back in my life, those memories are infecting me. Like the time I threw a rock at a wasp nest then ran like hell. That's how this felt. Those memories catching up to me every time I was around her. Just like wasps stinging me over and over again that day. I knew better than to let her in. She was a piece of normal to me during a difficult time, while I was trying to navigate the chaos of my mother. We aren't the same dumb kids we used to be. It was just a phase, and it's better to pretend she never existed than to wonder if she ever cared at all. If she had, she wouldn't have worked with Bryan to set me up.

I'm about to leave when something catches my eye. The bracelet she's wearing. She notices where my eyes are focused and glances down. I grab her by the wrist and pull her into me. She doesn't pull back, and I lean into her. My lips brush over her jaw, then up, as I whisper in her ear, "Goodnight, Mariah."

Chapter Nine

Mireya

I open up the apartment to see Alma's cat, Don Chee-tos, stretching on the couch. Alma didn't have to work, so she stayed at Thalia's and slept off her hangover while I rushed to my Friday morning classes. I could barely sleep last night after Adrian left. He called me Mariah. Again. And when he pulled away and saw my face, I could have sworn he was holding back a laugh. He's playing with my head. I know he saw the bracelet he gave me. He remem-bered.

I start a load of laundry and start a pot of coffee. If I am going to study through the night, I am going to need all the energy. Alma usually cooks dinner on Friday nights, and that would give me more time to study. I need to focus on school first and then worry about whatever is going on with Adrian.

As if she can sense my distress and needs to add to it, I get a call from my mother. I hit the ignore button, too tired to deal with her verbal assaults and passive aggressive remarks. Constance Torres only calls me when she needs some form of entertainment or someone to gossip to about the Consuelo Family. I hate the way it makes me feel to listen to her made up stories about the family, when they treat me far better than she ever did.

"It looks like Adriana Consuelo got a nose job. She should have done something about those hideous eyebrows."

"Why does Olivia Consuelo never smile? I heard the twins' dad left her because she was always nagging."

"How did Thalia lose all that weight? Is she sick?"

And on and on, her obnoxious questions go, her jealous vile spilling all over the place. Projecting her insecurities onto me. Once the call goes to voicemail, I pull out a palo santo stick Alma had given me for Christmas and light it. I circle the sacred stick over my phone as if it will get rid of my mother's attempt to drain my energy.

Every time I answer one of her calls, it is the same thing. She talks and talks until the conversation inevitably ends with me defending myself and telling her I don't have time to worry about what other people did or didn't do with their lives. She would hang up, and within minutes,

I would receive a text accusing me of caring more about the Consuelos than my own mother. It's exhausting, and I don't have time for it today. I could go months without speaking to her.

If she wasn't talking about the Consuelos, then she was talking about my father's family. She would even go as far as to call him names without thinking about how it affected me.

I miss him so much. He always carried the weight for my mother when it came to parenting. He was at every open house, he supported my hobbies and encouraged all my dreams.

"Anything you want to do, you can do, Gordita. You just got to put your mind to it."

I hated when kids made fun of my weight, but when my dad called me Gorda, it was a form of endearment. If I told white people my dad called me fatty, they would probably put me through rounds of therapy, but some words didn't translate directly. His family was from Jalisco, and my grandmother would make this sweet bread, gorditas de nata. They were my favorite, and in true Mexican fashion, it became my nickname. I smile, thinking of his voice. I needed his encouragement now more than ever.

I study for the rest of the afternoon and well into the night. I barely hear Alma get home until I hear a knock at my door.

"I made some Caldo de Pollo," she says softly, and when I open the door, I notice her eyes are red and puffy. She is an empath, so I know she's sensitive, and anything from a lost dog flyer to a sad song makes her cry, but this feels more serious.

"You okay?"

"I don't know. I'm about to start my period and Adrian gave me a letter the other day and I have just been really emotional about it." Something like jealousy builds in my gut before I shove it down. "That guy is such an asshole."

"He wrote you a letter?" I ask, still trying to piece together how they would know each other.

"No. I don't even know him, but he is connected with someone from my past. Someone who has now recruited Adrian to be his messenger and guard dog. The letter was from him."

"I'm sorry, Alma. Just don't read the letters, and we'll have Thalia talk to Adrian."

"I texted you earlier today to tell you I saw him talking to your mom in the front lobby." *Shit.* I had been deep into studying. I sometimes go days without checking my phone. I run to my room and grab my phone off the bed.

Sure enough, I have six more missed calls from my mother, the text from Alma, and several texts from my mother.

"*Mireya, why aren't you answering me?*"

"*I guess I'll have to go to the hotel and make sure the Consuelos haven't killed you.*"

"*Do you still have your restaurant pass for the seafood buffet?*"

"*Why did you not tell me Adrian Ibarra was out of jail and WORKING with you?*"

She must have run into Adrian while looking for me. It was Friday, and every Friday the restaurant sets out an all-you-can-eat seafood buffet. We all have free passes once a month for the buffet. Since I hate seafood, I usually give her mine.

I should have answered her earlier. As much as I hate to do this, I decide to give her a call to figure out what she said to Adrian. She picks up on the first ring.

"Nice to see you can remember your own mother."

"Hi, Mom. Sorry, I've just been really busy with school and studying."

"Yes, and I'm sure Adrian has been a part of that really busy schedule." Her sarcasm is like nails to a chalkboard. An entire Palo Santo tree couldn't get rid of this woman's negativity.

"He just started working there. We barely see each other, and I'm not sure he even remembers me," I say, that familiar anxiety building up in me. Ready to start defending my every life choice.

"Oh, he remembers you. He recognized me immediately," she says before she rambles on about her hate toward Enrique Consuelo. I let her drag on for a few minutes before I find the perfect exit strategy and hang up.

I go back into the kitchen to eat with Alma and pick up the dishes. She knows how heavy the conversations get with my mother, so she doesn't pry into it. We lounge in the living room and watch a few episodes of Vampire Diaries as we both try to wind down from everything going on around us. My mind is in another place. I need to call Adrian out on his bullshit. First this dumb little game of pretending he doesn't know me and then the fucking letter he gave Alma. I can tell she's still shaken up about it, especially if she, of all people, doesn't want to talk about it.

Chapter Ten

Adrian

I wake up to a knock on my door. I look out the peep-hole and see Thalia standing outside in a fuzzy black robe and the most hideous monster-looking slippers I've ever seen.

I open the door and stare at her hideous looking slippers.

"Hey. I just wanted to say thanks for last night. Sorry I was so drunk."

I nod and go to shut the door, but she's already coming through it.

"You know we don't have to be the Shining twins or anything, but I would like to be civil and understand each other at some point. Especially if we have to work together. We're going to need to trust each other," she rambles on, then stops as she looks around my apartment.

"Wow. I can't believe how spotless this place is. There's

barely any décor. Where are your pictures?" she wonders out loud before looking at me. "Oh, right… prison. Sorry."

We look at each other and I can't help but laugh.

"Where did you get those hideous slippers?" I ask, and she rolls her eyes.

"Come on, Frankenstein, Olivia will cook us a top-notch breakfast, and I can tell you all my fashion secrets." She links her arm in mine and drags me out the door to her penthouse.

Within minutes, I have been introduced to Lucia and Luca. Lucia gives me an entire tour of their playroom and every toy in it. Olivia welcomes me with a simple hug. I like the way she invites me in but doesn't force the whole "long lost family" member thing on me or look at me with pity the way I sometimes catch Patricio and Enrique doing.

She makes us Chilaquiles, eggs, and homemade beans. Thalia has brought out a ton of family albums and is showing me a funny picture of a time she convinced Olivia to dress up with her for Halloween. Thalia is dressed as Nacho Libre and Olvia glares from under a nun costume.

"¡Pendeja!" Olivia huffs, and I start laughing.

"Don't let her convince you to dress up with her, Adrian. She always gets the spotlight, and you end up looking like an idiot. Always."

Thalia has moved on to show me her social media so I

can see more pictures of her Halloween costumes.

"Omg! We should make you an Instagram!"

"Osiel already made me one."

"Osiel is a pendejo," she huffs. "Let me see what kind of profile he gave you. What's your username?"

"I don't know. I just gave him my phone, and he set it up." I omit the part about how I only agreed to it so I could stalk Mireya and didn't pay much attention to anything else.

"Let me see." She grabs my phone, and I watch as she opens the app, then rolls her eyes as she shows me my profile.

"Your username is BigDickAdrian?" Olivia starts laughing from the kitchen where she is cleaning up.

"Fuck," I say as I run a hand over my face. "Please help me change that." She laughs, then continues to do something on my phone, when she stops to look up at me. At first, I think she's going to ask about all the porn stars Osiel followed, but when she holds up my phone, it is on the Instagram search page with Mireya's profile as the first suggestion.

"Were you Instagram stalking my best friend?" Her eyes narrow on me. I'm going to punch Osiel for not mentioning search histories in his stalking course.

"I like the word 'investigate' better, but I also learned a

long time ago not to speak without a lawyer present." Her brow arches.

"So, you do know her, then? You know her name is not Mariah." I let out a small laugh. I got the idea after I heard a customer call her that, and it was too amusing to watch her not correct them. I could not pass up the opportunity to mess with her head.

"She hasn't told me anything about you. Just that you grew up together. I had a feeling it was something more, though. Call it... sibling intuition."

"I was her boyfriend before Bryan," I admit, and only because I figure I can use this to my advantage and see what information I can get out of Thalia. Judging by the look of disgust on her face at my mention of Bryan, she has a lot more to say.

"Bryan was a real piece of shit. I never knew him when they were together, but when I did meet Mireya, she was still pretty fucked up from the whole thing."

"Fucked up, how?"

"Well, I think long term it created a bunch of insecurities. He broke up with her for—" she stops, realizing something. "Oh, my god. You were the ex who dated Diana!"

"What about Diana?"

"So, get this. Bryan and Mireya had made plans to go to

prom together, and when he didn't show up, she decided to go, anyway, but when she got there, he was with Diana."

Interesting. That made sense, considering she was the prime witness in the defense's case against me. Diana was likely his accomplice.

Thalia notices my silence, but doesn't push, as if she knows my revenge plot already. She leans forward and holds her head up with her palm.

"You know they are having an engagement party here, at the hotel? It's next month, but I bet we can lure Bryan here sooner." That familiar crazy look on her face matches the one on mine. She is stirring up her own revenge plan. We might be more alike than I thought.

After breakfast, I make my way to the front desk to see what needs to be done for the day. Enrique fired Don Mario for drinking on the job again. He was trying to hand out pajaretes for breakfast when one of the maids snitched on him. At least he was thoughtful enough to share the drink with others. He was from a small ranch town in Mexico, where the drink was more common. It was a strong mix of coffee, chocolate milk, and vodka. I would have taken one if I were down there. Who am I to refuse the hospitality of my elders? This would be the third time Enrique tried firing him this week. He'll be back tomorrow.

Thalia had worked on narrowing the addresses Patricio gave me down to one, where she suspected my mother was located. I had a few days off before we planned to raid the place.

I am working on changing out lights in the main lobby when I see a familiar face walking in. Constance Torres, Mireya's mother. The bitch never liked me, and I never liked her either. She would often come by when my mom was home, inviting her for nightly walks, but she always came off as fake. She's dressed like she's been invited to the royal palace, and I watch as she walks up to the reception desk. She must be looking for Mireya, who even I know doesn't work Fridays. *Investigating, not stalking.* She is about to turn and leave when she recognizes me descending the ladder.

"Adriano?" she says as she walks toward me. She has on a fake smile to match her fake designer heels. "Adriano. Mijo. ¿Como estas?"

As much as I want to ignore her, I also know the game I need to play. Consuelo may know where my mom is, as most of the neighbors have confirmed the last time they saw her, she was getting into Constance's car.

"I'm good, Mrs. Torres. How are you?" Enrique and Patricio are coming in from a meeting they left to when they spot me talking with her.

"Constance," Patricio says as he approaches us. He greets her with a hug and kiss to the cheek. She stands there for a second, waiting for Enrique to do the same, but he just stands there, looking at her with disgust written all over his face. If she notices, she acts unbothered as she turns to Patricio.

"Adrian used to live in my neighborhood. Well, before he went to jail for drug charges." Patricio smiles, unphased by her attempts to insult me.

"Oh, but don't you worry, he is such a nice kid, and I'm sure he learned his lesson." Before I can even reply, Enrique's tongue is armed and ready.

"I'll have you know, Con-stan-ce," he says, drawing her name out to three syllables, "that Adrian is our nephew. An heir to the luxuries of Calavera Hotels." He opens his arms to the lobby, waiting to see her reaction. She looks unamused by this news, but not at all surprised. *Interesting.* Maybe my mother had confided in her about my biological father.

Constance makes up some excuse about a high society brunch before leaving. Patricio sighs as he looks to Enrique. "Do you have to be such an asshole all the time?"

"With her, yes. She is a snake wearing fake Gucci heels. She only came here so she could harass Mireya into giving her a Seafood Buffet pass." He rolls his eyes as he walks toward the office.

"Your Tio Enrique, the diva of Calavera Hotel," Patricio says with a chuckle and follows behind him. But Enrique is on to something, and while I thought I could do this job alone, I may need to bring Thalia in on my revenge plan and get what information I can out of her about Constance Torres.

Chapter Eleven

Mireya

"You were sleepwalking again last night," Alma says. I decided to catch a ride with her early to work. I could hang out at Thalia's before I started my shift.

"Was it bad?" I ask. I've had sleep problems since my dad passed away. I slept a lot during the first few months. I would have vivid dreams of him, and in my distress, the dreams were all I had to look forward to. My mother's solution to the problem was to slap me every time she caught me walking around the house, crying for him. She had me see a doctor, but his best remedy for the problem was lowering my caffeine intake, monitoring my stress levels, and avoiding alcohol before bed. All of which are not happening anytime soon with the shit going on in my life.

"Well, you were eating all the gansitos from the freezer and..." she pauses, and I watch as she tries to think.

"And what? Just tell me, Alma!" I hope I hadn't attacked her again. She was too sweet to tell me if I had. The first time she and Thalia found me sleepwalking, Thalia tried to wake me up and I attacked her.

"You were asking Adrian to fuck you," she whispers, as if someone could hear her through the car. I throw my hands into my face as I lean back into the seat and groan.

"Sex dreams are absolutely normal." In typical Alma fashion, she tries to comfort me. I'm grateful I share an apartment with Alma and not Thalia. Had it been Thalia, I'm positive I would have been recorded and mocked for years on end.

"Maybe you are just sexually frustrated?" That is an understatement. More like I am sexually depriving myself. I hadn't even touched a vibrator in the last year. I even thought about asking Doctor Aguilar to prescribe me something for my libido, but I am too embarrassed to bring it up. Yet, ever since Adrian came back, it's like my libido was miraculously resurrected. The day he pushed against me, the rough way he grabbed my wrist, and the quick looks I would steal when he was around. The other day, I had to call him to unclog the women's bathroom in the lobby. I was turned on watching him plunge a toilet, for Christ's sake.

I've had several sex dreams since he returned. I would

wake up wet, with the smell of arousal on my fingers, like I had been masturbating. God, I hope I wasn't masturbating in front of Alma. I had read about sleep walkers developing sexsomnia, but I also read it was more common for men. I didn't think anything of it, much less that it would affect me.

"What am I going to do?" Alma's resolution is to hook me up with one of the other maid's brothers. She's starting the long list of all his good qualities and their entire family history.

"What did you say his name was?" I might need to take her up on the offer. At this point, I needed to get Adrian out of my mind. By June, I could quit my job and never see him again.

"Osvaldo." The name sounds beautiful in her Spanish accent. It would never sound like that coming from me and my broken Spanglish. Another of my many insecurities.

"Wait, isn't that Oswald in English?"

"Ya. I think so."

"Alma, I can't date a guy named Oswald. The name Oswald makes me think of Benjamin Button as an old man baby. I wouldn't be able to look at the man without thinking about him aging backward on me and having to hold him like Cate Blanchett at the end of the movie." It's shallow and petty, but this is usually why I didn't date to begin with. I always find one thing that makes me dislike the person. I joined Chispa once, and there were plenty of attractive men on there, but I would find one thing wrong and block them. Alma sighs and turns up the music. I'm a lost cause.

When we get to the hotel, I make my way up to Thalia's apartment just as Olivia is rushing out the door.

"Hey! Oh my god. I'm so glad you're here. Can you watch the kids for a few hours when Thalia leaves? Beatriz is sick." Beatriz was Doña Clara's daughter, who usually watches the kids. They are good kids, so I am content with helping out.

"Yes! I got you!" I yell down the hallway and watch her get in the elevator.

Thalia is cleaning the kitchen when I let myself in.

"You should have been here yesterday. Adrian came over for breakfast," she singsongs Adrian's name, like a childlike taunt.

"You guys are having morning brunches now?" I say, half annoyed about my lack of sleep and half jealous I wasn't invited.

"¡No seas celosa! I got chisme for you!"

I stare at her. I am not jealous. The less time I spend around Adrian, the better. I have enough problems with my self-diagnosed sexsomnia. I am curious what juicy details she had about him, though.

"What's the tea?"

Her eyes light up with her signature sly smile. I usually do my best to avoid any forms of gossip, due to my mother traumatizing me with hers. However, if Thalia has information on Adrian, it could be beneficial to my overstimulated ovaries. If I'm lucky, it will be something revolting to me, like the many men I found on the Chispa dating app. My shallow mindset would attach itself to that one revolting thing, and in return, my libido would go back to its resting state.

"I guess Osiel, of all people, helped him make an Instagram profile. He put his username as BigDickAdrian." My cheeks flush. Adrian's dick was absolutely the last thing I needed to be thinking about. Let alone its size.

"He had no idea, and neta, he begged me to help him change it. So, being the amazing big sister that I am, I helped him." She waves her hand. Thalia often went off subject or exaggerated stories. I was afraid another hour would pass by before she got to the main point.

"Anyways, that's not the point. Dude, you'll never guess the first name that came up in his search history." She pauses for dramatic effect.

"It was you!" she screams like an over-pepped cheerleader.

"Really? So, he obviously remembers me. You should have asked him why he was pretending not to know me. And then ask him why he just glares at me every day. I can't tell if he wants to kill me or fuck me."

"Oooh!" she exclaims. "Maybe he wants to do both." Then she laughs when she sees the horror on my face. I wouldn't be surprised if Thalia spent her free time reading erotic horror or visiting fetish clubs. There's no way in hell I'm going to tell her about my sexsomnia problem now. It's bad enough Alma had to witness it.

"Maybe this is how we become sisters for real."

Heat rushes up my face at the thought, and I'm thankful when Lucia barges in and asks if she can do my makeup. Unable to say no to her cute little face, I say yes and figure I'll wash it off before my shift starts. Thalia leaves to her office and I make the kids lunch. Luca is extra cuddly today and I fall asleep on the couch with him.

When my phone alarm goes off, I still feel tired, but I hear Olivia in the shower and the twins are still napping, so I slip out and make my way down the elevator. The lady next to me in the elevator doesn't stop staring at me, and it's making me nervous, so I rush out into the lobby. I need to get my uniform from Alma's car before she leaves for the day. I'm halfway through the main lobby when I see Adrian on a ladder, hanging a banner. He is looking at me again, but more puzzled than his regular glare. Having enough of this walking on eggshells bullshit, I decide today, of all days, to be brave.

"What the hell are you staring at, Adrian?"

A smirk draws on his face and he gives me no response as he climbs down the ladder. He's wearing a white wifebeater, his muscular frame on full display. There is little left to my imagination as I stare at the outline of his abs through the thin material. The view will likely result in more wet dreams. I'm frustrated and still a little grumpy from my nap. When he reaches the bottom of the ladder, he still has that puzzled look on his face. Anger builds in me.

"I don't know what your problem is, Adrian, or what games you're playing with me. If you want to act like you don't remember me, fine! But if you have something you need to get off your chest, then just say it instead of giving me dirty looks every day!"

He moves into me, and my breathing picks up as he shortens the distance between us. I can already feel the heat between us. My heart pounds as he pushes my hair behind my ear. The touch a jolt of electricity to my core. He lowers his lips to my ear, his voice barely above a whisper.

"I'm staring because you look like a fucking clown."

I pull back. Confused and angry. *A clown?* He grabs

the ladder to leave and just as I go to tell him to fuck off, I catch my reflection in the lobby mirror. My hands shoot up in embarrassment as I remember letting Lucia do my makeup. I run to the parking lot and jump in the passenger seat and pull the visor down to get a closer look at the dramatic workings of a six-year-old upon my face. I groan as I see the bright pink and purple eyeshadow, bright orange blush, and the clown-red lipstick that completes the look. It doesn't help matters that when I fell asleep, I smeared most of the lipstick up my cheek. I wonder how much it would cost to change my identity and move to another country.

Chapter Twelve

Adrian

Freshman Year of High School

I was getting tired of making up excuses for my mother. By age ten, I was making calls to her employer so she wouldn't lose her job. Most times, out of pity for me, they would give her another chance. And another, until she ran out of chances. I was also good at pacifying teachers when she couldn't make it to the various meetings they requested her to be at. Those meetings about my violent outbursts on the playground. Socializing was never a skill of mine, however, it had always been a primal need to earn respect.

Back then, the excuses worked. Her binges wouldn't last longer than a few days to a week, but now it's been a month, and if I don't get money fast, then we will be evicted. I've spent the last three summers working for Romero's Lawn Services. It helps, but the pay barely cuts it when we are behind on all our bills. When the oldest Romero brother offers me a little extra pay to run drugs for him, I don't even have to think twice.

I am supposed to meet Mireya at our local meet up spot tonight. It's an old abandoned clubhouse one of the earlier tenants built for his kids before the neighborhood went to shit. The new owner of the house has no kids and works all night, so the clubhouse was ours. I'd been avoiding her more in the few months since I started working with the Romeros. Recently, I've started skipping school so I could make more money. She's noticed, but never says much. I stopped calling her as much as I used to. Even looking at her makes me feel guilty for what I'm doing. The part of me that wants to be a better person for her. It's as if she expects the world from me. My safe place. However, the more I struggle to survive, the more I see how ruthless I can be.

The pent-up rage from my mom's addiction often makes me question my own worth. It isn't like I woke up one day and said, "I think I want to be a drug dealer when I grow up." No, I am a lost cause. Where Mireya glamourizes me, people like the Romero brothers see the struggle. They knew it would lead to ambition they could use and we would all benefit.

In all my attempts to try to save my mother, I fell into a dark hole, addicted to the violence and power offered to me on the streets. It was the only place I felt I had control of my life. I convinced myself that as soon as I could move up my street game, I would find a way to make sure she was taken care of. I would find a way to help her slaughter all her demons. And in my delusion, I was convinced I would have time to make it right with Mireya.

When I get to the clubhouse, I wait for an hour, and Mireya never shows. It's not completely unlike her, and it's possible she never got my note. Our cellphones had been turned off again, so I make my way back to my house. I would swing by tomorrow while Joaquin was at work. He wouldn't let Mireya out of the house right now if he was home. She usually had to sneak out to meet me, but Constance might have caught her again.

I'm surprised when I get to my house to see her there–Constance, sitting on my front porch, smoking a cigarette. The lights are off, so Mom is likely still not home, or if she is, she's sleeping off the binge.

"My mom's not here." I walk up to the porch. Constance has never liked me and more so once she found out how much time Mireya and I had been spending together.

"I didn't come here for her. I came to talk about my daughter and you."

"What's there to talk about?" I cross my arms over my chest. I heard the way she spoke to Mireya when Joaquin wasn't around. She was no better than the kids who had bullied Mireya at school. That is, before I stepped in. The day I caught some kids throwing rocks at her was the first time I released all my anger. I broke one kid's arm and left the other bloody on the cement. Mireya stood there and watched me as I fought them. I thought she would run away, but she stood there and waited for me. Wrapped her arms around me afterward in gratitude, and it was the first time someone had done that. I was determined to keep her.

One of the parents threatened to sue me, but Joaquin had stepped in when he heard what I had done. He thanked me for helping her and then threatened the parents that he would sue for harassment if they touched me. None of us in this neighborhood could really afford a lawyer, so nothing happened. The kids stopped harassing her, and I made sure of it by walking with her every day. The more I talked to her, the more I couldn't help but find her company enjoyable. I had spent fifteen years of my life feeling like I was alone, but she always found a way to make me feel included. Asking questions about me and not about my mother.

"Mireya has a lot of potential," Constance says as her eyes scan me up and down. "She has a lot of opportunities. Opportunities she won't take if she's shackled to you."

"Shackled to me?" That familiar blaze of red makes its way up my neck. The anger ready to surface.

"I see you running around these streets. You and I both know the type of life you can offer her. The same one that keeps your own mother gone for weeks on end." The comment burns me. She watches me as that anger builds back up in me. Who the fuck does she think she is to talk about my mother? I stalk toward her.

"Get off my fucking porch," I growl and push past her to open the door.

The next day, I told Mireya I couldn't be with her anymore.

"I don't understand. You're breaking up with me?"

I could see the hurt in her face, but I didn't sleep the entire night, Constance's words repeating over and over in my head. I needed to survive more than I needed a girlfriend. I also questioned where my life would be. I was old enough to know fairytales didn't exist in the hood. I couldn't risk Mireya's chances of getting out of here. I couldn't risk being the thing that held her back. So, I did what any dumb fifteen-year-old boy would do when she asked why I was breaking up with her, and I pointed out her flaws. I told her I wasn't attracted to her, that it was me, not her, and whatever other bullshit word vomit I could come up with.

She had tried for the next two weeks to reach out, but I continued to shove her away. When her father passed away, it took everything in me not to look for her. When I heard she had gone to Arizona, I was hopeful that she would get the opportunities Constance had thrown in my face. It wasn't until I walked into a house party and saw her in Bryan's lap that I felt the weight of losing her. In the end, I was responsible for her running to Bryan, but it didn't stop me from hating her for trusting someone like him. It didn't stop me from hating myself for letting her get away.

I sat with that anger. I knew I would need it for tonight. Thalia, Ricky, Osiel, and I are packed in Thalia's SUV. We had gotten a lead on a house that sat on the outskirts of Houston, hidden on an abandoned farm. Thalia is sure that my mom is there. Conejo and his men trail behind us in the van for backup.

"Turn off the lights," Thalia says to her driver.

The road leading up to the house is dark as we make our way to the farm. We are armed and ready. The adrenaline pumps through me. Even if my mother isn't here, we are prepared to get the other women to safety and kill anyone who objects to that.

As we get closer to the farm, I see only a few men standing outside, guarding the house. Ricky rolls down the window and starts firing at them. It doesn't take much to dismantle their security and make our way inside.

I rush in with Osiel behind me. The entire house is chaos after the gunshots they heard outside. Men run from the back rooms as they try to dress themselves.

"Who the hell are you?" a woman says, a shotgun pointed at our men. Her face matches the face of the pictures Thalia had shown me when looking for evidence. Several women who had been rescued remembered seeing my mother when they were held captive here. This is the woman who would groom them, drug them, and find suitors for them.

Osiel rushes toward her, and her shot hits the ceiling. When Thalia rushes in, I can see the fury in her eyes, and she slams her gun into the woman's face. I fire shots at the men coming out of the room. Other than the guards at the entrance, there are very few security measures inside the house.

Ricky has already blown off two guys' heads who were sitting on the couch, blood splattering the girls who were forced to entertain them. They scream, and he yells at them to go outside. The entire scene makes me sick. Some of the girls look barely older than Lucia. I make sure to kill every piece of shit sitting in the living room, waiting for their turn to torture one of the women. Cries ring out from the back rooms, and I move toward them.

A young girl, barely ten or eleven, runs out from one of the backrooms. Thalia rushes toward her and grabs her. Ricky rushes to the room she ran out of, and I hear rounds of shots fired. When he comes out, he is covered in blood, his face filled with fury.

The upstairs rooms are set up and cleaned for clients. All of them are now emptied and covered with blood. I make my way slowly down the stairs to the basement to find another room set up with multiple beds. I put my finger up to my lips to warn the women to be quiet.

"I'm not going to hurt you. Help is on the way." I point to the stairs, and they take off, running up them. I see three rooms and motion for Osiel, who is behind me, to check them. The doors are locked from the outside, so we have to work fast to kick them in. The first room I reach has several women trapped inside. No beds or furniture. The entire basement smells of sweat and urine. None of the women are clothed, and they are dirty, lying on the floor. I can see their dilated pupils, and they barely register my presence with all the drugs they have been fed.

Osiel helps to get the women up the stairs. I can barely make out faces, and I don't have time to figure out if any of them is my mother. We move them out and check the house thoroughly before setting it on fire. Thalia had already set it up so the police we worked with would make their way over and take the women somewhere safe. They have already arrived and social workers are making their way to help the women.

"Soledad," I scream out. My voice is hoarse, but I keep calling her name, searching the faces of the women.

"Adrian!" I hear Thalia scream from the back of an ambulance. I run to her and the woman beside her, covered in a blanket. It's my mother. She doesn't look the way I remember, but I know it's her. Thalia's eyes are bloodshot as she holds my mother. She has the same dilated pupils as the other women I ran into. Her face is blank and bruised. I grab her and bring her close to me. "Ama," I say, and tears flood my eyes. "Ama, we're going to get you out of here. I'm so sorry. I'm so sorry I left you." I kiss her forehead and wrap my arms around her.

She is quiet the whole ride home. She hasn't processed that she's been rescued. I should have let her go with the trained professionals, but I couldn't risk losing her again. When we get to the hotel, we drive around back where Patricio is waiting outside, pacing back and forth. He rips open the door immediately and pulls my mom to him. "Soledad."

She breaks down in his arms as she begins to cry. A part of me hurts at the sight. She hadn't recognized me when I approached her. But she clings to Patricio and cries into his chest. Darkness draws in, and I feel like that little boy again. The one who, deep down, knew she hated him for being born.

Chapter Thirteen

Mireya

I've spent the entire week doing clinic work and studying for upcoming tests. Thankfully, after the clown incident, I didn't see Adrian again. It's midnight and my eyes are heavy. The lines on my textbook are starting to blur. Don Cheetos is meowing, and I hear the tv on in the living room. When I walk in, I see Alma is fast asleep on the couch, so I cover her with a blanket and head back to my room and lie down.

I decide to look for the profile Adrian had set up. I go through Osiel's page and smile when I find it. There are no pictures, but his profile picture is one of him in some black shades with a smile. He had an authentic smile when he showed it. Full lips and perfectly straight teeth. There is a nagging part of me that wonders if he is even single. Thalia hasn't mentioned anything.

That insecure part of me decides tonight, of all nights, to look up Diana's profile. Her username is *futuremiss-mendezxo*. *Gag*. Her entire identity is her relationship with Bryan. All her pictures, an online shrine of the two of them. Each one with a paragraph-long caption, talking about how perfect he is and how happy she is.

I have seen most of these pictures before. It is usually my go to activity to stalk her during my downward spirals. I can't very well master self-sabotage if I don't compare myself to the girl who both my exes favored after being with me. While healthy women sought therapies or get revenge bodies, I just dig a bigger hole for myself to hide in.

Diana is girly and flirty and fun. At least, her Instagram page tells that story. There is not one single picture on her page where she doesn't have her hair curled and her face fully glammed. I look down at the Tapatio stain on my scrubs and groan. I wouldn't date me either. I'm about to look up makeup tutorials when an incoming call comes through. I read the name GAEL. It's Doctor Aguilar's personal number.

"Gael?" I whisper. Calling him by his first name outside of the formalities always feels weird, but he had insisted I stop calling him by his title outside of the hospital.

"Mireya. Hey. I am on my way to the hotel. Something's

come up. Can I pick you up?" Alma and I usually share a car, and Gael lives close by, so he usually just picks me up when he is called out in the middle of the night like this.

"I'll be outside." I know this routine well. I grab my medical supplies, throw on a new shirt, and slip on my Vans. I text Alma, in case she wakes up and I'm not there. She is convinced there's something more to my relationship with Gael, and I let her imagination run wild so I can avoid her questioning. When I get outside, I see him waiting for me at the curb.

"This is going to be different than what you're used to seeing. I want to prepare you before we get there." I already figured as much since we were going to the hotel. Usually, we are called directly to Patricio's estate, or Conejo's ranch, when there is a medical emergency. Something about tonight feels off, and I'm not sure I am prepared for what is coming.

When we get to the hotel, I see Thalia pacing the front entrance.

She rushes towards us. "Thank you both for coming." There is panic in her eyes, and I can see the blood stains on her clothes.

"What's going on?" I ask her, as we follow her through the quiet lobby and into the elevator. Gael had told me about the women they rescued. I couldn't imagine what she had been exposed to prior to seeing us. Her eyes are red and puffy. When she goes to speak, her voice cracks. She gives Gael and me a brief summary of the events that had happened earlier that night. I am barely able to keep up after she mentions Soledad.

I shake my head in disbelief. I had known Adrian's mother. When they first moved to the neighborhood, my mom had befriended her. They would go on nightly walks, often dragging me and Adrian along with them. That was how I met Adrian. He hadn't acknowledged me much on those walks, but he always seemed protective over his mother. When we did become closer, I rarely saw her and he rarely mentioned her. Never once did he tell me she struggled with an addiction.

"Patricio has been looking for her for the last few years, since he found Adrian in jail," she explains. "I need to warn you before we go in there, Mireya. She's not okay. And Adrian is murderous right now. Don't take anything personal."

"Mireya, I want you to follow my lead," Gael says. His voice is softer. He's speaking to me as a friend, not as my superior. "I have dealt with these scenarios before, and if you feel like it's too much, let me know right away, and I will have someone take you home."

When we get up to Adrian's penthouse, Thalia opens

the door. Patricio is still in his work clothes; his hair is disheveled and his tie is loose around his neck. He stands as soon as we approach him.

"Thank you both for coming on such short notice."

Adrian is pacing behind the couch, and my eyes move from him to the woman lying on the couch, covered in a blanket. Her eyes are blank as she stares off into the distance. She has lighter, softer features compared to Adrian. Adrian and Thalia look a lot alike, but there are similar features he shares with his mother, too. Those same features are now marked with dirt. Her hair is tangled, her eyes red and swollen like she hasn't slept in days. Not the same beautiful woman I remember. She looks broken and lost. My heart aches at the sight of her.

When she sees us enter, she sits up and looks around. Adrian's eyes meet mine, and the rage consuming him is visible in the glare.

"What the fuck is she doing here?" He looks at Patricio, who frowns at him.

"Calm down, *Adriano.* Mireya is at the top of her class in nursing school, and Doctor Aguilar will only work in her company. We need to work in silence, and a trip to the hospital could jeopardize your mother's safety." His tone is calm and firm. I look to Gael.

"I can leave."

"If she leaves, then I leave," Gael says to Adrian. Gael has dealt with Adrian's type before. Anytime he is disrespected, he pulls back immediately. He has gained respect amongst the Consuelos, and he is a necessity in their dark world of violence.

Fury burns in Adrian's eyes. He won't back down from Gael–I can see it–but then he looks to his mother. He begins speaking in Spanish, as if trying to call her back to reality. Back to him.

"Soledad, do you remember Constance?" Patricio asks, and her lifeless eyes meet mine as she nods. "This is her daughter, Mireya. She's going to help you to the back room to examine you, and then we will clean you up. Thalia, can you get her some clothes?"

I grab my supplies and do a basic assessment, trying to be gentle as my hand goes over every bruise and wound. My heart breaks, and I want to cry, but I keep it together. I can't even begin to imagine what this woman has been through. I stay professional, knowing it will build trust with her for when we need to move to the bigger inspections. I ask everyone to leave as Gael instructs me on how to do a rape examination. I hold back my tears as I follow his every instruction.

Her soul is wounded–I feel it–the same way my own has been wounded. The work I've done with Gael has never been this intense. We mostly deal with bullet wounds, or broken bones, but this is different. As soon as I'm done, Gael takes the samples he needs to make sure she doesn't have any STDs or an unwanted pregnancy. She trembles under my touch.

"Breathe, Soledad. It's just me. It's Mireya. You are here, in this moment; you are safe, and you are cared for," I say and repeat the mantra over and over to remind her that we are in the present, to remind her that she is safe. Something I learned from an empath lecture one of my teachers gave my first year of nursing school.

Sometimes, it just took a kind voice, a mantra, or affirmation to ground you. Words that provided you with a small light in the dark tunnel of your mind. Right now, it is just me and her in this room. A nurse and a patient. The markings of her drug use run along her arms and toes. I touch each one, as if some healing power will radiate out of me. As if I can take the pain away from her. Eventually, she looks up to give me a broken smile.

I walk her into the living room and sit next to her and hold her hand. Adrian never takes his eyes off us. When Thalia returns with some clothes, I ask Patricio to help me get her into the bathroom. He goes to pick Soledad up off the couch.

She wraps the blanket around herself as he lifts her up

and carries her into the bathroom. I start the water and she sits on the toilet, her face blank. She's trying to make sense of all this. I can tell, with the disorientation written all over her expression. Gael will have to run more tests to figure out what drugs were in her system. I repeat my mantra to her, "Breathe, Soledad. It's just me. It's Mireya. You are here, in this moment; you are safe, and you are cared for." I look up to see Adrian watching me. His arms are crossed as he leans on the frame of the door. I want to reach for him and comfort him.

"Do you need help?" I ask her, motioning to the bathtub. Everyone leaves to give us privacy, and she nods her head slightly. I shut the door and help her into the bathtub. There is woman empowerment and then there is this. This raw feeling where you see the scars of another woman and you can feel everything they are feeling in that moment. You understand how truly little you are in the eyes of a society that claims you the weaker sex. My fingers move gently as I use a sponge to bathe her. By the time I have helped her dry off and into some of Thalia's PJs, Gael has set the room up for her.

"Let's get an IV going. I don't need any test results to see she is extremely dehydrated," he says to me, and I help with the IV. Once we have her set up and comfortable in the bed, Patricio makes his place in the chair next to her. He and Adrian have had it out several times about him taking her to his estate. I know Patricio has a private staff that can care for her 24/7, but Adrian refuses to let her out of his sight.

I am beginning to pack up my medical supplies when Patricio shoots up from the chair.

"Mireya, please, can you stay the night tonight? Just so we have someone on hand?" He runs his fingers through his thick brown hair. His green eyes are pleading, his face exhausted.

"I don't know if that's a good idea." I look to Adrian, and his eyes meet mine. We stand there for a second. I know they are all worried about her, but I don't want to make Adrian uncomfortable.

"You can sleep on the couch." I can see the torment in his eyes as he walks away. I want to follow him. I want to wrap my arms around him, tell him how I messed up, and figure out how to be there for him the way I need to be. I want to talk through what the last six years have been like for me. How much I needed him at one point. How I underestimated Bryan's plans that night. I never wanted to hurt him, and I need to make things right.

Chapter Fourteen

Adrian

I can't sleep. I thought I would be able to once I knew my mom was safe, but I hadn't realized how stressful the process would be. Images from that farm where they kept her appear every time I close my eyes. Young girls drugged and disoriented. Even in prison, if we found out grown men were hurting children, we would cut their fucking heads off and all play basketball with them. Even criminals like us loathe pedophiles.

But I know my mother is safe now. Patricio refused to leave, and she seems more content to see him than me, so I didn't fight him on it. The same way I didn't fight him over the busty brunette sleeping on my couch. When she looked at me tonight, I could see the pity in her eyes. *Poor Adrian.* I don't want her pity. Not when she played a part in my incarceration. To be honest, my anger has no landing point right now. I am pissed at everyone who had been in that room. I am mad at Patricio for not protecting my mother from his brother, mad at Mireya for letting Bryan use her as an alibi, and mad at myself for being born. I hated the way that doctor stood up for Mireya, and I had wanted to reach out and rip his heart out of his chest. He was the exact person I had envisioned her with when I let her go. The type who could offer her the world, and yet I still can't see her with anyone but me. I hate myself for that, too.

Watching her with my mom made me want to stop this push and pull game with her. They are the only two women I have ever cared about. I can see why Patricio asked her to stay. I know she cares about my mom, and not just because she's a nurse, but because she cares about this family. *My family.*

I look at the clock on my end table and I see it's 4AM. I throw the blankets off me. Trying to sleep at this point is useless. The penthouse is quiet, and I need a cigarette and something to eat.

I'm mouth deep into some corn flakes, trying to stay quiet, when I hear footsteps coming from the living room. I reach for the gun in the back of my pants but stop when I see her. Mireya is walking around the living room in her bra and panties.

What the fuck?

This is exactly why I didn't want her to stay. I knew it would be awkward, but I didn't think in a million years she would be stripping down and walking around my penthouse half naked. She bumps into the couch but keeps walking towards me. I'm already prepared to ask her what the fuck she's trying to do when I notice the deranged look on her face. As if she is a zombie, mumbling but detached.

Holy shit. She's not... sleepwalking, is she?

One of my old cell mates would strip down to his whitey tighties and wander the halls. He had been locked up most of his life, and the senior guards were aware of the behavior. They would warn us not to wake him. He would get violent if we tried, but as long as nobody woke him up, he would eventually wander back to the cell on his own. Other times, they would gently guide him back to his bed. He was already prone to violence in his waking state; no one wanted to see what a disoriented version of him looked like.

Mireya walks past me with her eyes open, but barely acknowledges my existence. I check down the hall to see my mom's room is closed. Patricio is in there, and I don't want him to see her like this. She walks to the patio, and I am right behind her as she makes her way to the pool. She sits on a patio chair, and when I move to face the front of her, I have to do a double take to make sure I am seeing this clearly. She is sitting on the edge of the chair and her legs are spread wide. She's mumbling something, but I can't make out what she's saying, so I move in closer.

"Adrian."

"Adrian."

"Fuck me, Adrian."

My spine straightens.

Hijo de su chingada madre. Motherfucker.

Did she say what I think she said?

My dick sure as hell heard that as it grows beneath my sweats.

I don't have time to tell it to calm down when I see her striding in a seductive way right towards my pool. I run my hand over my face as I watch her plump breasts bounce. She's walking on her tiptoes, like she's walking a runway in heels. I can't help but laugh. If I had my cellphone, I would record this shit. Blackmail her with it. I step in front of her. She stops, like she can see me, but her eyes are glazed over. She's still stuck in whatever erotic dream she's in. I gently turn her around, so she is facing the penthouse. The touch of her skin doing nothing for my hard on, and I pray Patricio stays in that room. I doubt any of this looks innocent. Her half dressed and my hard on. She barely registers my touch and stands still. I move to the front of her to see if she is finally gaining consciousness. My eyes roam over her red lace bra and the see-through panties, her cunt glistening under the Texas moon light. We are only a few inches away when she runs her hand over her breasts. It's seductive, and it only gets better when she runs that same hand into her underwear and begins to massage herself. Her hand palming her shaved pussy as her middle and ring finger slide in and out. My eyes are glued to the movement. The moon continues to shine on her, the brisk air hardening her brown nipples under the thin material. She looks like a goddess, and sounds like one, when she begins to moan. The sound is low and sweet. The long syllables ringing out, an invitation to join her. I grab my erect dick and begin to pump it at the same speed. Back and forth, back and forth. I can hear her wetness as she moves her fingers quicker. What kind of sex demon comes out of her at night if she's masturbating while she sleepwalks? Does she do this every night?

I start pumping my cock faster, my strokes matching hers. I pull up my shorts just in time to catch my cum shooting out. She's breathing deeply as she tries to catch her breath from her own self-induced orgasm. Then, like nothing happened, she walks back into the penthouse. I follow behind her but guide her back to my room. There's no fucking way I'm going to chance her walking around like that with Patricio in the other room. I guide her into my bed and whisper for her to lie down as she continues to mumble. She lies down effortlessly as she returns to sleep, but not before I hear her murmur again. "Fuck me, Adrian."

Chapter Fifteen

Mireya

When I wake up, I am in complete dismay. I'm IN ADRIAN'S BED! I'm in Adrian's bed in my bra and panties. Oh, and to make matters worse, my panties are soaked. *What the hell happened?!* I look over to see my clothes neatly folded on the side table beside me. I panic more when I see the clock. It's a little past 8AM, and I quickly begin to get dressed. *Shit, I must have been sleepwalking again.*

I don't know how I got here. Did I fuck Adrian last night? Oh my god, what if I tried forcing myself on him? Images of me breaking into his room, sex deprived and unconscious, flood my mind, and anxiety takes over. Worse than the anxiety is the fact that I'm slightly turned on by the idea. "¡Calmate!" I scream internally, hoping the message makes its way from my brain to my vagina. Assuming she speaks Spanish, since she obviously didn't get my English memos to stop lusting over Adrian.

I finish putting on my shoes and make my way to the door. I slowly open it, sending out silent prayers to any slut-shamed ancestors who could spare me this embarrassment. I peek down the hallway. The door is shut where Patricio and Soledad stayed. I listen and don't hear any sounds of Adrian in the house. He could have left already. I listen for a second longer before determining the coast is clear to run out. I have no time to do the walk of shame. I need to do a full-speed slut sprint out of here. I tip-toe to the hallway and double check the living room. It looks empty. I come up with my mastermind plan to shoot straight across the hallway, past the kitchen, and to the door before making contact with anyone.

I am halfway through executing my plan when I get to the kitchen entrance and run right into Adrian. The cup of coffee he was holding now all over the front of my shirt. I gasp, and he moves to grab some paper towels.

He's shirtless, and my eyes can't help but to stare at his muscular back and the large portrait of a skeleton woman that covers it. *La Santa Muerte*. I've seen her candles at Mr. Friborg's Botanica. The detail on the tattoo shows her adorned with flowers, angels, and a banner that reads "Protect Me".

When Adrian turns back around with the paper towels, he immediately presses them against my chest. I stiffen and his eyes drop to mine. "I'm sorry," I say, as I look down to his hands as he soaks up the coffee. I'm overwhelmed by the sensation building in my nipples and the heat between my thighs. His muscles flex, and I'm sure he's sensed it as his movements stop and he holds the paper towel there on my sensitive nipples. I do everything to not look up at him. Instead, my eyes wander back over the designs on his stomach and down to that deep V at the top of his sweats. I look down further to see the outline in his sweatpants. He's hard.

"Picking up where we left off?" he says as a grin appears on his face.

My cheeks flush.

My eyes shoot to find an exit. "Abort mission!" I scream to my vagina as I run straight to the door.

Chapter Sixteen

Adrian

I head to the shower after Mireya leaves. A very cold shower. I don't have time to take care of my dick, and at this point, we've come to an agreement that Mireya is worth waiting for. After last night, I've decided she will be mine. Her dreams are mine, her moans are mine, and her punishment will be mine to carry out. The plan developed while I watched her sleep next to me. It was something about the way she drifted back to sleep. The softness of her face, her chest rising and falling with each breath, and her pouty lips mumbling my name. She was as desperate for me as I am for her. I need to have her. I need to punish her for what she did and remind her who she belongs to.

I get dressed and make my way back to the kitchen when I see my mother and Patricio sitting at the table. She looks better than yesterday, but Dr. Aguilar said it could take a month before we get all the drugs out of her system. Patricio spreads jam over a piece of toast for her. He is still in his clothes from last night. They both look up when I walk in to take a seat at the table.

"Ama, how are you feeling?" She looks up and offers a faint smile.

"I'm good, mijo. I'm tired, but I'm happy to see you." She reaches across the table and her hand grabs a hold of mine. She looks up to the ceiling, trying not to cry. I have witnessed her like this a dozen times. It had been a cycle every time she used. She was always sorry, but only until the cravings returned. Then she was desperate and using again. As if he can hear my worry, Patricio looks to me.

"We need to find a more suitable place for your mother to recover."

"I wasn't talking to you. I was talking to my mother." I stare right at him as my jaw clenches. He wants to take her to his fancy estate, with his staff and luxuries to keep her busy. He wants to be her knight in shining armor. *Over. My. Dead. Body.*

"Your mother needs help, Adrian. I'm not saying she has to come home with me, but she does need to be around professionals. I can find her a high-quality rehabilitation facility, where both her physical and emotional needs can be assessed." He's not backing down.

"You're not her fucking savior, Patricio." I'm not back-ing down either.

"Adrian. Patricio is right. It might be better if I go with him until I can check myself into a facility." I look at my mother's exhausted face. Her voice soft and her eyes pleading.

"No! This family shut you out! And you think you're safer around him than you would be around your own fucking son? If you hate me so damn much, just say it!" The words fly out like bullets.

She stands up and reaches over the table and slaps me across the face. I immediately feel the sting, her hand sharp against my face.

She stares at me, and I see where my words hurt her the most as tears fall down her eyes.

"I am the one who told Patricio to get me out of here. How do you think it makes me feel to have my own son see me like this? To see me weak and broken. I was supposed to take care of YOU! I am your mother, Adrian, and I was supposed to take care of you." She breaks down and sobs as Patricio moves to comfort her.

There's a strange feeling pulling in my chest. It's like I'm that ten-year-old boy again. The one who put so much pressure on himself to rescue her. The loneliness I felt as a child and the promises I made myself to never feel that weak again.

"Ma, I'm sorry. I just—" I can't find the words, and my voice cracks at the thought of her leaving me again. "I just want to help you."

"I know you do, but you can't do this for me. I have been running for so long, and I am tired, Adrian. I've spent every day since you got locked up regretting the person I've become. The type of mother I was to you. I have let the past control my present, and I don't want it to control my future."

"There are dark things in my past that I have been running from for far too long. Things you are old enough to understand now, so we can take the next step forward. So I can take the next step forward. The first thing you need to understand is nothing that happened to me was Patricio's fault. I hid things from you, and I hid you from them." I give her my full attention. It's the first time she has ever talked openly about her addiction.

"I was afraid of your biological father. What he did to me broke me, and I had no way of escaping what he did when I was carrying his child. I didn't want you. I tried to tell my mother, and she didn't care. As a devout Catholic woman, she would not entertain any other option." She squeezes Patricio's hand tighter. Her face is blank, like retelling this is a step toward finally staring her demons down. I was her demon.

"I'm sorry." The words fall out as a plea. This whole time I had been trying to save her, she had been running from me—the embodiment of her trauma. This whole situation is fucked up. I was forced on her. Something she never wanted. The ache in my chest tightens.

"When I saw you, Adrian, my feelings changed. I was selfish. I wanted to keep you. I wanted you to save me. Patricio was ready to raise you as his own son, and I saw light at the end of the tunnel. He was willing to give all this up. It was a hard decision, but at the time, I thought it was better for me to do this alone. I didn't want Patricio to sacrifice anything for me. I knew I'd destroy him in my sadness. I pushed him away, and I leaned on you. I'm sorry for that. I never wanted you to grow up feeling unloved, but I could never give you the love you deserved."

I want to be sad. I want her to love me. I want to be angry. I want to die. I want everything and nothing, all at once. I watch as tears fall down her face, and all I can think about is how damaged I really am, but she was allowed her truth. Even if that truth shattered me. There it was. I had never been loved, and I would never be able to love anyone. I want to think about her, but I've spent my whole life thinking about her. I was a little boy, working harder on her recovery than she ever did, just so she would love me, and in the end, it did nothing. I would always be a reminder of my father.

"Adrian, are you okay?" Patricio asks.

"Don't worry about me. You did your part already. I don't need shit from you or you," I say, as I point to each of them. "I loved you, even when I had no idea you could never love me. You fucking tore me apart, and I still went to the gates of hell to find you. I see now that may never be enough."

"Adrian, please don't be mad at me for speaking my truth."

"Go. Get out! Let Patricio save you and forget I ever existed!"

"Adrian!" She stands in protest, but I'm already out the door.

I need to get the fuck out of here. I see where she is coming from, but it doesn't make it hurt any less. I never knew what I was expecting in finding her. That I could make her love me. Nothing I did would ever matter to her because I am still the son of a monster. It's not only her that looks at me like that, either. I see everyone and hear the whispers. They are worried I will be as ruthless as my father. Why not give them what they're waiting for?

I am halfway into a bottle of Patrón when I hear a knock on my door. I spent most of the day walking around to clear my mind before stopping by the liquor store. I had several missed calls from Patricio, followed by a text message.

Patricio: We just left. We need to talk when you're ready.

I take another sip of the liquor and let it burn down my throat. When I open the door, Mireya stands and takes me in. I watch as her eyes observe the darkness in the house. The darkness in me. She takes a step in. That's her first mistake. She must not have gotten the memo to steer clear of the devil's bastard. She notices the empty room in the back and looks at me as I take my seat on the couch next to my bottle. Peso Pluma's version of *Fuentes de Ortiz* blares from the speakers behind me, and I pull out a cigarette as I stare at her.

"I don't think they allow you to smoke in here."

"Ask me if I care."

Her eyes shift, and she nervously scratches her arm. She's still in her work uniform, but I haven't been able to get the images of her from last night out of my mind. The way her fingers slid in and out of her wet pussy. Her little moans as I pumped my dick. I want to take her to my bedroom and tie her up so she can never leave me. So, no one can ever leave me again. I stare at her and blow out the smoke in a satisfying exhale.

"Is everything okay?" she whispers, taking in the half empty tequila bottle on my coffee table.

"I don't know, Mireya. Why don't you tell me?" I say, giving her a long, hard stare. I am tired of the bullshit games we are playing, tired of trying to figure all this shit out on my own. She had a part in that setup. I want to see if she is willing to own up to it or hide behind a lie. I want to rip all the band-aids off today.

"Maybe we need to talk, Adrian."

"Great. Let's start with why you lied and said you were with Bryan the night I got arrested? Or why don't you tell me why your mother was the last person seen with my mother?" Her eyes shoot toward me and her eyebrows furrow.

"I... didn't know about my mom." She rocks back and forth as I stalk closer. My six-foot frame towering over her.

"I had no idea what Bryan was doing that night. I didn't

know you were involved until it was too late. I was... I was just doing what I was told," she says, looking up at me, her pouty lips trembling and her eyes searching mine.

"And you're such a good girl... Do you always do what you're told?" She backs into the wall and I cage her in. My knuckles tracing along her jawline and slowly grazing down her neck, over her pulse, that familiar vanilla scent overtaking my senses. I let my knuckles roam to her breasts and stroke lazy circles around her nipples. Her eyes shut as she takes in the sensitive touch.

"Do you think I deserved to be punished for something I didn't do?"

"No," she says in a raspy breath.

"Do you think you should be punished for lying?" I grab her breast and squeeze it.

She arches her back and whimpers. All fear washes from her face, replaced with something that will damn us both–*desire.*

Chapter Seventeen

Mireya

I'm staring into Adrian's eyes. My hands move to the bottom of his shirt, and I lift it over his head. My pulse races as I reach a hand out and run my fingertips over the tattoos covering his bare chest. I lick my lips as I find the hardness of his abs. He sucks in a breath at the delicate touch. My silent response to his question.

Do you think you should be punished for lying?

Maybe I should. Maybe my body has been craving this release. Craving him. He can see it in my eyes. He pushes into me, and I back up into the wall as he slides a hand down the front of my pants. To the throbbing between my legs. He growls into my ear as he places a finger inside of me. *Santo Dios.*

I go to look away, but he grabs my face, turning my attention back to him. His brown eyes filled with the same heat as his touch.

"Eyes on me."

I stare back at him, and he adds another finger. I adjust as he stretches me, thrusting his fingers inside. My breathing picks up with the movement. I can hear the wetness, and my pussy clamps around him, begging him to stay there. I'm on the edge of letting the sensation overtake me when he pulls his fingers out.

His eyes stay locked on me as he brings his fingers up to his mouth and sucks on my arousal. I'm frozen in place as I watch him. He removes his fingers and uses them to nudge my lips open.

"Taste how wet you are for me."

My lips part, and I stick my tongue out as he glides his fingers in. I close my mouth around them as I taste myself. His fingers fill my mouth, and I moan around them.

"Good girl." Those two words gasoline to the flames in my heart. My tongue chases after the taste of his fingers, and I lick my lips when he removes them from my mouth. He wraps a hand around my throat, and my hands move to his.

"Take off your clothes." His tone is authoritative and rough as he releases me. My hands shake at his intense glare. I pull down my pants and remove my shirt. There is something intoxicating about the way he is looking at me.

He hisses in approval as I stand before him in my black lace bra and thong.

"Una diosa." He moves back into me and presses his lips into mine. He kisses me savagely, biting on my lips and wrapping my hair into his fist. I can feel his hardness through his sweatpants; his thickness grinding into me.

He picks me up, and I wrap my legs around him as he walks to his bedroom. He continues to devour my mouth. His hands holding my ass, squeezing me into him. My hands wander to the back of his head as I push myself deeper into the kiss. He bites my lips and moves to my neck. I dig my nails into him as he sucks hard on the sensitive flesh. He drops me onto the bed, and I push myself back onto my elbows, watching the fire in his eyes consume me.

"Get on all fours." My nipples harden at the command. I do as he says and get on all fours as I face the headboard. He strokes a hand over my pussy. The thin material of my panties is soaked. When I feel a sharp sting, I catch myself from falling forward. I don't have time to register it before I feel it again. Another gentle caress, followed by a hard slap to my ass. He repeats the motion as I cry out. The pain mixed with pleasure taking over me. Again and again. I push my ass back, needing more, as my clit throbs for his touch.

"You're such a naughty girl. Do I need to punish you more, or do you think you learned your lesson?" His hand stops and lingers over my ass as he caresses me. When I don't answer, he strikes again, harder, and the slap echoes in the room.

"Punish me!" I cry out through the pain, needing more. My body rocks back and forth, desperate to meet the sting of his hand, my clit pulsing with each caress. Over and over again, before my thighs clench, and I'm screaming into the pillows as the orgasm slams into me, my body set on fire and blazing through the depths of my soul.

He turns me around and stares at me as I let the flame of my orgasm die down, his body hungry with desire. He drops to his knees and pulls my legs to the end of the bed. In one motion, he rips off my underwear.

"I want to taste every last drop of you."

He lowers his mouth to me. He's aggressive as he sucks on my clit and bites at my folds. I let out a moan as he feasts on me. Another orgasm builds in my core, but he pushes off me.

"I need to feel inside this tight pussy. Are you on birth control?" he asks, and I nod.

"Good, because I'm going to take you raw." He pulls down his pants, and I see his length and girth. I've never felt so aroused.

I spread my legs, ready to accommodate his size. To have every inch of him filling me up. He pushes in and stretches me, the pain setting another fire deep in my core. I want to feel him deep inside me. I want him to set me on fire. He moves in slowly. His crown stretching me open as he fills me. He throws my legs over his shoulders and pushes in deeper. I meet him with each thrust, my orgasm starting the climb as he thrusts into me. Hot liquid makes its way down from my core as he thrusts harder. That familiar heat ready to break out like a forest fire, consuming everything in sight. I scream out his name when the orgasm blazes through me. I feel his cum filling me like hot lava. Flames bursting around me. Blinding me.

"Diosa," he whispers into my ear as he collapses on top of me, rolling us to our side, his softening dick inside me. My body shutting down from multiple orgasms, I wrap my arms around him and close my eyes as I let the fire of him consume and drift into sleep.

Chapter Eighteen

Adrian

I wake to feather-like touches on my back. Mireya's soft touch exploring me and picking up where we had left off. We woke up various times throughout the night to feel and explore one another. I couldn't get enough. I turn over so my eyes meet hers. She is so beautiful. That first hit of her was exhilarating. The feel of being inside her was my very own form of destruction. Losing her once broke me, but I don't think losing her again would work in anyone's favor. I am too ruthless, too raw, and too broken to let her be happy without me. I am the worst thing for her, but I don't care. She was always supposed to be mine. I reach out and cup her face.

"If you keep doing that, we're going to go another round."

She bites on her lower lip and hides a smile. She brings

her hand to mine.

"When did you get the tattoo on your back?" She's talking about the large Santa Muerte tattoo I got while in prison. I had forgotten the last time she saw me I was ink-free.

"About two years after I was sentenced."

It had been a dark time. Before I even knew about The Consuelos or made my way into Los Antros. I was tried as an adult, but mentally I wasn't prepared for the shit that went on in that place.

"One of my first cellmates was a Santa Muerte devotee. He talked about her like someone I knew. This dark presence that had followed me but never hurt me. She was there to protect me when I was younger. One time when I was eight-years-old, my mother didn't come home for a few days. The house was dark, and I was hungry. I felt La Santa Muerte in that moment. Before I knew who or what she was. It was darkness and fear, and yet there was comfort in it."

"La Santa Muerte," she whispers as if afraid to say it but curious to understand it. "I never knew about your mom. About—" I press my finger to her lips.

"Shh... Ya. I didn't want anyone to know. I don't want anyone's pity," I say as I move to find my pants.

"I felt like that for a long time, too—alone and lost.

Sometimes I still do." She comes up from behind and wraps her arms around my waist, her bare chest on my back. It's the first time in a long time I feel whole, but I can't give myself to her. I know better than to trust anything anymore. Not when my own mother could see the monster inside of me. I turn around to face her.

"Any image you have of me in your mind, you need to shatter. I'm not that same person." She looks into my eyes, and where I thought I would find hurt, I see understanding.

"I don't think either of us is."

After Mireya leaves, I do my daily workout routine, then head down to Enrique's office to see what he wants me to do for the day.

When I walk in, he's sitting at his desk, drinking a large cup of coffee. The mug in his hand reads "Antes muerta que sencilla." It fits his personality. Enrique Consuelo would much rather die than show up anywhere looking simple. His fitted Prada suit and Rolex are evidence of that.

Thalia stands, looking out the ceiling-to-floor window. She has her hair up and is wearing her signature color of all black, with dark makeup to match. She looks up at me and smiles. The devilish grin a taunt, like she knows something I don't. Knowing her, she must have seen Mireya leaving my penthouse this morning and has been waiting to confront me about it. I ignore her and make my way into the office.

Enrique gives me his once over as he examines my outfit.

"Adrian. My favorite sobrino, sit down." He gestures to the seat in front of his desk and I sit down. He hasn't known me long enough to consider me his favorite nephew, but he wouldn't pass up an opportunity to get under Thalia's skin. She rolls her eyes and moves to the seat next to me.

"What's this about?" she asks, her voice slightly annoyed.

"I wanted you both here for this. I have been doing some digging into Constance." He holds our gaze, pausing for dramatic effect as he continues.

"Now, I love Mireya dearly, despite her fashion sense, and I know Thalia does as well. So, as much as I hated Constance and her fake designer wearing ass, I never tried to dig deeper into what she was up to. She's always been like a cucaracha around here, but it's time we bust out the Raid."

"I'm missing my hair appointment because Constance offended you with fake designer clothes?"

"No. I was concerned she had something up her sleeve. The way she was looking at you, Adrian–I did not like that. So, I called my resources, and sure enough, she's up to something. One of the valets told me she was calling someone and talking about Adrian. So, I pulled up the camera footage for that day." He turns his laptop around to show us a video on the screen. When he presses play, a panicked Constance dialing a number on her phone fills the screen.

"Adrian is out, and he is working at the Calavera Hotel," she says into the phone. She's panicking and asking the recipient how I got out and how I figured out I was related to the Consuelos? I can barely make out the rest of the conversation.

"Who could she be talking to?" Thalia asks.

"That's what I'm trying to figure out. I sent the footage over to Patricio, so he knows, but I want both of you to keep an eye out for her."

I need to keep an eye out for Mireya. Figure out what her relationship is like with her mother. It wouldn't be hard to hack into her phone and see if they have been plotting something together. She very well could be the one Constance called. For all I know, they could both be trying to set me up again.

Chapter Nineteen

Mireya

After classes, I meet Alma for lunch. I texted her the night before that I was staying at Thalia's, but I knew Thalia enough to know she had already told the world she saw me leaving Adrian's penthouse this morning. I wouldn't put it past her to pay for a large billboard announcing it to all of Houston. When I get to the taco truck, Alma is already sitting at a table with her plate.

"Have fun at Thalia's?" She smirks, and I roll my eyes. I know she wants details. That's how we are. We love to hear each other's stories of failed dates and spicy hook ups. Well, mostly just Thalia's stories. Alma barely goes on dates, and I haven't even hooked up with my vibrator in months. Thalia claims I have become a virgin all over again. That my hymen closed up and grew cobwebs on the front with a caution sign. The same caution sign Adrian forged past multiple times last night.

I order three tacos and an horchata and make my way back to Alma, who is all too eager to get the tea. Her eyes go wide as I recount the details of the savage way Adrian fucked me. She gasps in horror about the spanking and gasps again when I admit to her how much I liked it.

"Was that how intense it was with Bryan?" The name alone ruins my meal.

"I don't think I even knew what an orgasm was with Bryan. At least from what I can remember." I grimace. I really assumed my experience with Bryan and his friends was the extent of sex, which is why I avoided exploring it. I didn't need someone just humping me like a rabbit while I lay there, bored on my back. Now that I've been with Adrian, I could easily become addicted to it.

"So, what's going to happen now?"

"I honestly don't know." I sigh. "All I know is I'm worse than Rosie. I could walk into a room full of Ritchies, and I'd still pick Bob." Alma laughs. She lives for a good *La Bamba* reference. She was usually the one making them.

"As long as he doesn't hurt you, like Bryan, then I support you. Don't pressure yourself to make it anything more than sex."

She was right. I'm not sure if this will lead to anything other than that. A lot had happened since I'd seen him last, and it was a lot to unpack for both of us. I'm still not sure why Bryan had set him up or what my mom had to do with it.

"I feel like he's closed off and private about his life. It may never go past anything more than sex, even if that's what I want." I frown at the thought.

"Well, then, it runs in the family," Alma says, her expression shocked, as if the words weren't meant to be spoken aloud.

"What is that supposed to mean?"

She looks down, so I ask again, "Alma, what are you talking about?" Her cheeks flush red at her mistake.

"Oh my god. I'm sorry. I don't want to be a chismosa, at least not when it comes to my friends, but I am really worried about Thalia."

"Thalia? Why would you be worried about Thalia?"

"I never brought it up because I would love her regardless, but I once heard through maid chisme that Thalia had been pregnant and went to California. They say when she came back, she never brought the baby back."

"That's a touchy subject, Alma. Not just as her friend, but as a woman, I trust she did what was best for her."

"I know, and I would never judge her. I never paid attention to the rumor because I felt the same, but a few days ago, I overheard Doña Clara and Enrique talking about someone blackmailing her." Her brows furrow, and I can see the worry etched in her face.

"What do you mean?"

"I mean, someone is blackmailing her, and I can't help but think it has something to do with the whole pregnancy thing. I don't want to bring it up because I don't think she knows. Doña Clara has been covering it up."

"Whatever it is, Alma, you have to stay out of it."

"I know, but Thalia was there for you with Bryan, and she helped me with everything with my mom. Maybe we can help her with this?"

"I don't know. There must be a reason she never told us, and we need to leave it at that."

We finish our tacos and write out a grocery list for the week. I'm walking back to the hospital trying to piece together what she told me. I wish Thalia could trust us as much as we trust her. She genuinely cares about what we are going through and wants to help us in any way she can. That's one reason I trust her so much, because I know, at the end of the day, she will be there for me. I'll never forget the day her dad died, and she told me she felt so relieved. I could only imagine what happened to make someone happy to see their own father dead.

Chapter Twenty

Adrian

I'm walking around, doing maintenance in a few of the rooms, when I see Bryan walk in. Thalia had messaged me earlier to let me know he was going to be here, but I wasn't sure if I would actually see the motherfucker. He's wearing a suit and walking like a stick's been shoved up his ass, his hair combed to the side. I laugh to myself. He's changed, but not by much. He still looks like the same *hijo de papi* he's always been. The golden boy living off Mommy and Daddy's fortune. I watch as he meets his parents in the lobby, and they walk together to the event venue.

The venue has several doors you can use as an entrance. I peek through one and watch as Enrique shows them around the place. I get closer, so I can hear what they're saying, but just as I move to another entrance, I realize I'm not the only one trying to spy. Mireya is hiding behind one of the doors, and she looks nervous as she tries to listen in.

Rage washes over me. Why the hell is she still concerned with what Bryan is doing? I walk over and she looks up when she hears my footsteps. She backs away from the door and walks toward me.

"Adrian. What are you doing here?"

"I work here. What exactly are you doing here?" I cross my arms over my chest and wait for her reply.

"I was just looking for Enrique." *Lies.*

"I'm sure he's in here," I say and walk toward the door, but she stands in front of me.

"No. It's okay. I'll find him later."

"What don't you want me to see?"

"It's nothing," she says, as she starts that nervous habit of playing with her bracelet. I wrap my hand around her throat as I push her into the wall.

"Are you lying? You know you get punished for lying," I growl.

There's something about the way her pulse beats beneath my hand. Her eyes bulge as I tighten my grip, and she shakes her head furiously as a whimper escapes her mouth.

I drag her down the hall to a utility closet. I was just in there, so I know it's empty, and if I'm lucky, there are ropes.

"What are you doing?" she asks once I close the door

behind us and lock it.

"Why? Are you afraid of me?"

"No." She bites her bottom lip. "I know you would never hurt me. At least not intentionally."

"Really?" I watch her hands wrap around the stacked shelves behind her, using them for support, as I stalk closer to her. "Let's try this again," I say. "Why were you spying on Bryan? And don't lie to me."

Her eyes widen. I'm inches from her, standing toe to toe, and I can hear her breathing accelerate.

"I was just curious to see what he and Diana were planning for the engagement party."

"Fuck Diana and Bryan." I laugh maniacally at the thought. These two found paradise in bringing me down. The fucking audacity. At first, I'm pissed that they found happiness while I was in jail, but then something comes over me when I think Mireya might actually be jealous it's not her marrying Bryan.

"And you're jealous it's not you and the golden boy getting married?"

She shakes her head, but I'm not focused on her denial. I'm focused on her breathing and the way my body is reacting to her.

I slowly let my mouth graze against her jawline and down her neck.

"Adrian." She lets out a small moan, her eyes aligned with mine. They radiate with the same fiery lust.

"I'm going to devour every inch of you. I'm going to have you screaming my name, and when I'm done, you won't remember anyone's name but mine."

I pull her shirt up and rip off her bra. When her breasts fall out, I grab them. She's always been blessed in that department. Her tits are big and perky, and right now, they are all mine. I squeeze her nipple and she whimpers.

I grab the other nipple and pinch it. She whimpers again, but arches her back when I pull away. She wants more. The other night, when I was spanking her, she wanted more, too.

"Do you like when I punish you, diosa?" I bring my mouth down to her nipple and let my tongue circle over it.

"Yes," she moans. I take her nipple between my teeth and bite down gently. I want to mark every inch of her. I want every Bryan, Brandon, and fucking Benjamin on this side of Texas to know she is mine. I continue to suck on her nipples, her chest, and neck, leaving marks across her. Claiming what's mine. I pull down her pants and rip off her panties. She gasps, and I pick her up and set her bare ass on the metal steel of the utility rack behind her. She's completely naked in front of me. The body of a goddess.

I shove her panties in her mouth and reach for the duct tape above her. Her eyes go wide as panic fills her body.

"Shhhhh." I cup her face. "Do you trust me?"

She nods.

"Good girl. I promise you'll like this."

I find the rope I was looking for and tie her wrists to the bars of the utility rack.

"Breathe through your nose. If it gets to be too much, tap your hand against the bar and I'll stop." Once I have secured the restraints on both wrists, I scan her entire body.

"Spread your legs wide," I say, and she balances on her ass, spreading her thighs apart for me. A fucking masterpiece. Her shaved pussy is already soaking. I run my knuckles over her hard nipples, over her stomach, and then over her clit. I plunge my index and middle finger inside her and feel her wetness devouring my fingers. I slowly thrust them inside her as my thumb circles her clit. I can hear her muffled moans under the duct tape.

"You like that? You want another one, my little slut?"

Heat rushes to her face, and I add another finger, stretching her. She thrusts into them, begging and pleading like her body depends on it. Her arms fight against the restraints as she tries to thrust herself into my fingers. Her eyes begging me to make her cum.

"Not before I get a taste," I say, as I throw her legs up, angling her so her bottom half is tilted and the restraints pull tighter. I lower my head and lick her soaking cunt. She tastes so good. I was planning to take this slow, but her taste alone makes me mad with need. I scrape my front teeth along her clit, moving her arousal into my mouth. She is so wet. I squeeze her ass, bringing her closer. I can't get enough. The smell, the taste, I want it all.

She becomes feral, bucking and pulling on the restraints. I quicken my strokes, licking faster, plunging three fingers back into her and nibbling on her clit. Her body convulses as she rides my face. When her orgasm hits my mouth, I suck in every bit of it, eager to not miss a single drop. I keep licking and sucking on her clit as she rides out her orgasm. Her muffled cries filling up the room. I remove the duct tape and remove her panties.

"This is how sweet your pussy tastes," I whisper on her lips, then drive my tongue into her mouth. Our tongues swirl, and she's still panting as she tries to catch her breath. I remove the restraints and help her off the utility rack as her body regains composure.

"Adrian," she says through deep breaths. She leans against the utility rack behind her for support.

"Thanks for lunch," I kiss her forehead, and turn to leave, but not before I catch her ear-to-ear smile.

Chapter Twenty-One
Mireya

I'm trying to pull myself together, but my body is still in shock. For months, I've deprived it, and now it's had more orgasms than I can count in twenty-four hours. I use my phone to fix my hair and uniform. My bra is salvageable, but he took my panties, so I'm just going to have to roll with it. I head to the front desk and get back to work. I am deactivating keycards when I feel an unsettling presence behind me. I turn around and catch Bryan exiting the restaurant and walking toward the front lobby.

When he sees me, he looks around before making his way to the front desk. My heart is racing, and my hands start to shake. I have not seen this man in person since graduating high school, and even then, I made sure to avoid him and Diana as often as I could.

"Mireya. I didn't see you when I walked in," he says

when he approaches the desk.

Oh. My bad. I was getting head in the utility closet with the man you used me to help set up. Should have been waiting for you. I stare through him, and when I don't respond, he continues.

"Listen, I heard Adrian was out. You might want to be careful."

Well, too late for that.

"What do you want, Bryan?"

"I want to make sure that you keep your mouth shut about being my alibi." *Again, too late.*

"Your what?" I turn to see Thalia walking down the staircase. She looks at me and back at Bryan.

"I'm sorry, did I intrude on something?" She crosses her arms and stares at Bryan and me. Thalia doesn't know about me lying for Bryan the night Adrian was set up. I'm not sure this is the best way for her to find out either. Even if Adrian knows about it, she will see it as a betrayal.

"Nothing at all. Just checking on the party arrangements. Have a nice day." He winks at me and offers a fake smile before turning to leave.

Thalia is still staring at me.

"What the fuck was that?"

"Adrian already knows." I'm not sure why, but I feel defensive. She doesn't take her eyes off me, and I feel the disappointment radiating off her.

"So, he knows you and Bryan are still talking behind his back?"

"No. That's not what happened. You walked in at a bad time. I need to explain everything." Thalia does not do well with civilized conversation. She has always been quick to anger and quick to assume.

"Adrian is trying to get his life back on track. Don't fuck that up for him with whatever secrets you're keeping."

The words shoot straight to my heart as I watch her walk past me and to the elevator. *Don't fuck that up for him.* All the toxic thoughts start to take over in my head. Those feelings that I'm not good enough. Not good enough for my mother, not good enough for Bryan, for Adrian, and now, I am not good enough for Thalia. A five-year friendship that she would throw away to defend her long-lost brother. I am torn between being happy someone would stick up for him, and sad that she would see me as a threat to his happiness.

I work through the rest of my shift in silence. I'm grateful there's not a lot of people checking in tonight. I want to go home and crawl into my bed and forget this entire day existed. My anxiety is already working on convincing me, once again, to quit this job and change my identity.

Seeing Bryan again has me shaken up, too. He doesn't

scare me physically, but he always has something up his sleeve.

SOPHOMORE YEAR SAINT RITAS

Bryan picks me up from my house, and we drive to an abandoned alley by the train tracks.

"What are we doing?" I ask.

"I need you to pay off a debt for me." I'm not sure what he means until another car arrives and an older man gets out.

"Do you love me?" I nod my head and he gets out of the car. I watch as he approaches the stranger, then motions back to me. The man is much older than us and smiles at me as Bryan returns.

The memory is a traumatic experience that I had shoved so far down I never thought it would resurface. That was the first of many times Bryan would offer blowjob services to old horny men in exchange for extra cash to pay off his debt. The first time broke me, but over time, I became numb to it. Addicted to the toxic cycle when he would praise me afterward and buy me gifts. He knew exactly how to control and manipulate me.

It was crazy how a memory like that could unravel years of healing. I had been sure the emotional wounds he left in my soul were gone, but I could still see the scars. I want to cry, but I can't. Even as the tears build up and my throat aches, I hold it in. *You look ugly when you cry.*

My mother's voice comes back to me. I was never allowed to cry as a child. My mother would say it was distasteful and made me look ugly. Even after my father died, I had waited until after his funeral to lock myself in my room. I look at the clock and realize my shift was over twenty minutes ago. I had been so wrapped up in this sadness pulling me down. I planned on getting myself a drink before I call an Uber home. Something to take the edge off while I wait. I make my way to the bar, but then, as if I want another form of escape, I turn to the elevator instead, and make my way up to the thirteenth floor.

Chapter Twenty-Two
Mireya

I knock lightly, hoping he doesn't hear or isn't home. This is a very bad idea. All bravery has vanished, and a bit of anxiety has creeped in since I knocked on his door. I debate what I'm going to say, but he opens the door. He is shirtless, which catches me off guard. It's illegal for a man to look this good. But then I notice the icepack he holds to his cheek and the fresh blood on his lip.

"Oh my god, Adrian! What happened?" I move in to take the icepack from him and access the bruise before my eyes move to the open wound around his lip. I take off my jacket and reach for my backpack, where I carry some of my medical supplies.

"If you think this is bad, you should see the other guy," he says with a smirk. Arrogant asshole. I pull him into the bathroom and push him to sit on the toilet while I search through his cabinets for some cotton balls and peroxide. I had placed some in here when I was helping Soledad. I move quickly when I find them to soak the cotton in the peroxide. I touch it lightly to the wound around his lip. He grabs my wrist and yanks me on to him so that my legs are straddling him as he looks up at me.

"Thank you," he says, and our eyes stay locked on each other for a moment as he pulls my wrist to his lips and gently kisses the sensitive spot above my bracelet. The one he noticed me wearing the night he took Thalia home. The kiss is small, but it sparks that familiar flame inside me. The part of me that burns for him.

"What did you come here for?" he asks, his fingers gently playing with a loose strand of my hair. Suddenly the room feels hot. I don't want to talk about Bryan or Thalia. I don't want to ugly cry or confess whatever emotions I am feeling. I just want to stay here like this, in this moment with him.

His arms wrap around me, securing me to him, where I feel protected. I bend down and kiss him. Softly, I let my tongue search for his. He kisses me back. It's gentler than he's ever kissed me before. Slowly, we take each other in. The kiss is a heavenly offering to the universe that led us back to each other. Our tongues collide into each other as we pay homage to the stars that aligned to give this one last try.

He stands and lifts me, and I wrap my legs around his waist. He walks with me to the living room and drops me on the couch. We both tear at our clothes. Neither of us able to work them off quickly enough to appease the hunger. Our eyes never leaving the others.

"I need you inside me, Adrian." I unclasp my bra and let it drop to the floor. He growls as he removes his boxers as he stalks toward me. His dick is so hard, and a little bead of precum is leaking out. I moisten my lips. I want to taste him. I want to take him in and savor every taste. He can see the desire in my eyes and inches closer. I pull him into me. Wrapping my lips around his crown.

"Fuck," he growls and pushes in deeper as he grabs my hair. I slowly lick him and find a rhythm he likes. I look up and remove my lips and spit on his head. He hisses and pushes into me deeper as he places a foot on the couch. Tears pool in my eyes when he reaches the back of my throat. I hollow my cheeks and breath through my nose. He thrusts in harder and pain ripples through me the tighter he pulls my hair. I try not to gag as I keep my hands around his base, moving in synchronicity. I want him to cum in my mouth, to cum on my face and all over my breasts. Just when I anticipate his cum, he pulls out. I frown and he lets out a small laugh.

"Is my little slut sad I didn't cum down her throat?"

He sits on the couch and pulls me onto his lap. I slide down onto him as he stretches me. He grabs my waist and moves me upward. I follow his lead as he guides my waist up and down. I slide on and off his cock. He moans in approval, so I begin to circle my hips, trying to push him into me deeper. Something about the position, the control, I have never felt so aroused. He pulls his mouth to one of my breasts, and I arch my back as he thrusts from underneath. It's a sensory overload, his mouth sucking my tender nipples as he fucks me. I close my eyes as I feel that familiar bliss make its way up to my core. He grabs my hair, and my eyes shoot open.

"Eyes on me, diosa." I look into his as my drawn out moans become screams, and he grips my hips tighter. With one last thrust, our orgasms meet, and I feel his cum shooting up through me as he fills me with every last drop. We cling to each other as we ride out the high together. I collapse into him, my head resting on his shoulder as his arms wrap around my back. We stay there silent for a few moments when I hear my stomach growl.

"Did your stomach just growl?" Heat rushes to my cheeks. I can't remember the last time I ate.

He lifts me off him as he reaches for his sweatpants. I find my bra and panties and dress myself before he takes my hand and moves me into the kitchen. I sit at the table and watch as he removes a pot and some other ingredients from the pantry. The kitchen is cold, and my nipples are hard as goosebumps run down my arms. "Go in my room, and in the top drawer, I have some white t-shirts."

I walk toward his room, and I am surprised to see how organized he keeps his clothes. I didn't pay attention too much the last time I was in his room, but who can blame me when he was fucking my soul out of my body? My fingers skim over the top of his dresser. I look in the mirror to see the marks he's left on my chest and neck. My hair is a mess, but I feel good.

Gone are the memories that haunt me. Sex with Adrian is like drinking from the eternal well of life. I feel rejuvenated, alive, and back in control of myself. I grab a white t-shirt and slip it on. When I return to the kitchen, I can already smell the food he's cooking. My stomach growls again, which earns another laugh from Adrian.

He brings a plate of grilled cheese sandwiches to the table.

"Grilled cheese?" I ask, and he returns with a bowl.

"And sopa," he says, returning with a bowl of pasta shells in tomato sauce. My heart skips a beat when I see the classic from my childhood.

"My Tia Vicky used to make this for me. The sopa. Not

with grilled cheese, though," I say and smile.

"We're Mexican Americans. Grilled cheese is the best option for Sopa. We need the best of both worlds." He flashes me a sincere smile as he dips his sandwich into the soup.

"Okay, Hannah Montana. ¡Calmate!" I roll my eyes as I blow on the shells before I take a bite. I moan at the first bite. It tastes better than I expected. Adrian watches me from across the table, that same smile spread across his face. I haven't seen him smile like this since we were kids. It's warm and genuine. A softer version of him he had been only willing to share with me.

"Good?" he asks, and I nod as I go in for another bite.

"I learned a thing or two working in the kitchen at the prison. My homie, Efren, got really into it. I learned the basics of cooking before I had to focus on other things."

"I can't cook to save my life, but I do love to eat, and this here is five-star sopa."

"How does someone who loves to eat forget to eat?" His brows furrow, and I know he's not letting up on his original question from earlier. Why had I shown up on his doorstep, like Mary Poppins with my medicine bag, when I should be at home? I look down as I try to come up with a response. Deflecting failed, so I take my chance at sarcasm. It's the only way I can control my anxiety and emotions.

The man just gave me five-star sopa, and five-star dick. I don't want to ruin it with my emotional baggage.

"Well, I ate a protein cookie this morning, and we had clinics today, so I had to stay later. Then I rushed from school to work, and I was on my way to get something from the bodega when I saw Bryan." He frowns at me when I mention that part. "And then you tied me up while *you* had lunch, but I had to rush back to the front desk. Then Enrique had me write up Don Mario for drinking on the job again, and I had to deactivate a bunch of key cards. *Oh,* and then before Bryan left, he decided to come by the front desk, bringing up all the trauma I endured while dating him. Thalia scared him off, but not before she let me know I'm not good enough for you, and by then, I had lost most of my appetite." I smile to mask the tears that want to come out and take another bite. And the words of my mother help me keep it in. *You look so ugly when you cry.*

Chapter Twenty-Three

Adrian

"He did what?" I growl. Mireya is still trying to act unbothered about the entire situation, but I could tell the moment she walked in that she was not okay. I let her tend to my wounds and the sex for a distraction, but we aren't going to avoid the tough shit. Avoidance is the main ingredient in an unhappy relationship. *Why the fuck am I even thinking about a relationship?*

She looks down and moves her food around in her bowl, avoiding my question. I walk towards her and grab her chin, forcing her to look at me.

"Tell me what happened with Bryan." Her lips tremble and she looks away.

"What did he do to you?" I move to face her and take her hands in mine. I had forgotten how weird she gets when it comes to crying. When we were younger, she would hold it in or get up and leave as soon as she saw something that made her emotional. It was a good thing, I guess, for her profession, but not with me.

"Tell me what happened, so I can fix it," I say, and I mean it. She is nervous, but once the first tear falls down her cheek, she opens up. Telling me about the sick and fucked up ways he would make her pay off his debts, or humiliate her so he could show off to his friends.

He's a fucking little bitch. Any man who has to degrade a woman to show his authority is really just a fucking coward. He can't stand up to someone he knows would beat his ass, so he preys on those who are weak. I hate myself because I made her weak when I left her. All the bullshit I spat out, thinking I was helping her, just made her weak so that fucker could take advantage of her.

"Noone is ever going to hurt you again." I move my chair to her and pull her into me. She lets go of her need to hold it all in and cries into my chest. I refuse to shatter her soul again. I would much rather stick a knife through my heart. She doesn't need to say what I can see in her eyes when she pulls away from me. *Hypocrite.*

"There was a time in my life that I felt too damaged for you. I never saw breaking up with you as hurting you. I saw where you were going and the potential you had to be something. I didn't want the darkness that had sucked me in to follow you and suck you in, too." This time, it's me who's looking away, afraid to let her see that vulnerable part of me.

"I am never going to be the right man for you, but I can't stop whatever this is." My darkness would consume her. I know she will eventually see the monster I am and leave, but for right now, I need her to stay here with me. I slide my knuckle up her cheek and catch a fresh tear.

"I'm not afraid of your darkness," she whispers, her lips inches from mine. "We both failed each other. I made mistakes, too, but I don't want to lose you." Her hands are around my shoulders as her fingertips graze the base of my neck, caressing lightly. She leans in to kiss me, and I kiss her again, softer.

I want her to see this side of me. Let her see I can be her punisher and her healer. She needs to understand this balance. I'm willing to give her all of me. The light and the dark. The soft and the deranged.

She can't have the past version of me that she clings to without seeing the person I've become. I hold her in my arms a little longer before we make our way back to the bedroom. I pull the comforter back and move in next to her, pulling her into me and inhaling that sweet vanilla scent. I play with her hair until she falls asleep, and before I meet her there, I make a mental reminder to fuck Bryan's life up as soon as possible.

I'm waiting in the hotel lobby for Ricky to pick me up. Patricio texted to say he needs to talk in person, summoning me to his estate, which pissed me off because it means I won't be able to see Mireya tonight.

She has stayed the night every night this week. We've grown into a comfortable routine. Every night, she comes over, we eat dinner together, watch tv, and spend the night infused in each other. I even wake up early to drive her to her morning classes.

After Patricio ruined my night with his request to see me, I told her to take my truck and catch a ride home with Alma after work. I wasn't sure whether I would be home or not, and I didn't want her alone at the penthouse.

Mireya: Did I sleepwalk last night? (teeth clenching emoji)

Adrian: No. But if you ask me to fuck you again while sleepwalking, I'm going for it.

I already filled her in about the first night she stayed in my apartment, when she turned into a sex-deprived zombie. At first, she was embarrassed, but she admitted she wanted to try it. My little slut was aroused by the idea of me fucking her while she was asleep.

Mireya: You have no shame!

Adrian: Sleeping Beauty didn't mind.

She sends a Ted Bundy gif, and I can't help but laugh before I throw my phone in my pocket when Ricky pulls up. Patricio lives an hour from the hotel, and his property expands over twenty acres. On the property sits Don Vicente's house, Patricio's house, and active construction on two other homes, each at opposite ends of the estate. I'm not sure why Patricio never remarried or had kids, but I can only assume the additional houses are for the family he plans to have one day. *Hopefully not with my mother.*

To the far back of the property, closer to south-end, is the building everyone calls El Cuadrilatero, or El Cuadri, for short. Inside, there is a boxing ring, gym equipment, and an indoor shooting range. That's where I got the wound Mireya attended to, after Ricky and I went blow for blow, releasing pent-up energy.

I may have lied when I said Ricky looked worse than me. This fool didn't have a scratch on him afterward. The fucker could fight, and he loved violence. We all do, but I saw Ricky's eyes the night we found my mom. He was slaughtering every man on sight with a manic smile, like he was possessed. We get to Patricio's estate, and Ricky drops me off at Patricio's house, located in the center. The house is big, taking up at least ten acres of his property. It was a luxurious replica of the homes found in Mexico, with a modern hacienda design.

"I got some shit I got to do, but I'll be back tonight for you."

An older woman answers the door and leads me to Patricio's home office, where he and Conejo are waiting for me. There is a bottle of Don Julio 1942 on his desk, and they are both already sipping on the tequila.

"Adriano," Conejo says, relaxing on the green sofa. I move to sit on the opposite side of him as Patricio fills a glass and hands it to me. I haven't spoken to him since he took my mom to rehab.

"There's been a new discovery with Soledad." He looks at me briefly before looking away, but I keep my eyes on him as he continues. "They've found that she responds well with hypnotherapy. Every week, I have them record the session and forward it to me." He moves to turn on a big television that sits in front of us. I'd question HIPAA law, but this is the cartel's top financial advisor. Privacy is nonexistent.

When the video appears, and he presses play, I see my mom. It's been a few weeks since I last saw her, but already I can see the life and color that's returned to her face. I shift uncomfortably in my seat as I think about our last conversation. The hypnotherapist is counting her down into a state of calm.

"4, 3, 2, 1... and breathe. I am here if you need me. You are in a safe place," she says. I remember Mireya saying something similar to her. I smile, wondering if she's like that with all her patients. My smile fades. Hopefully not with the ones who have a penis attached to them. I look back up to the screen. The hypnotherapist is taking my mother back to the first time she used heroin—a memory to help with her recovery.

"Where are you, Soledad?" she asks.

"I'm... I'm in my house..."

"Good. What else do you see?"

"I... I just dropped Adrian off at school, and I am... I am waiting for someone," she says and looks confused.

Her breathing has picked up and her legs shake. The hypnotherapist comforts her, repeating the safety mantra to ground her.

"You are safe, Soledad. This is just a memory, and you are in control of it. Who are you waiting for?"

"I'm... I'm waiting for... for Constance."

"Who is Constance?"

"She is my drug dealer." Patricio watches as Conejo and I glance at each other. My mother goes on to explain that Constance was the first person to show her how to use it, to supply everything she needed, hotels to stay in, and money to loan her. My blood is boiling. I am going to kill this bitch. I stand suddenly.

"Adrian," Patricio says, snapping me back to reality, if only for a second. How can he be so calm?

"What's the plan, Jefe?" Conejo asks.

"The plan is, we kill this fucking bitch." I stare at Patricio. "I kill this fucking bitch."

"People who fly into a rage always make a bad landing," Conejo says as he sips his drink.

"I don't give a fuck." I will take both of them on when it comes to this. What did my mother ever do to Constance that she would want her to become addicted to drugs? That she would go so far as to supply her money. She couldn't have hated me that much. Patricio runs a hand through his hair. He knows what I'm capable of when I'm angry. That wild beast in me fights to break free. The murderous one that sees nothing but the power needed to rise to the top. The one who helped me make it through prison.

"It doesn't make sense. Constance has to be working for someone else. We need to string her along. Figure out what we can. I have my private investigator following her right now, and I have some friends at the Bureau pulling up her past to see if there are any convictions or connections. I wanted to let you know what was going on right away, but you can't act right now, Adrian."

I scoff. "You keep forgetting you're not my father. He's six feet under, and Constance will be joining him."

"I'm not trying to be your dad, Adrian. Do you want to run an operation like this? Do you truly want that revenge? Then take it from me: you have to buy time. Everything has to be set in place, and then once we know it's safe, we will strike hard and quick." His eyes burn through me. I know he's not wrong, but it still pisses me off.

"I'll call Adan and see if he can break through to her phone to track her movements," Conejo says.

"There's more we need to discuss." I pace, trying to get my rage under control as Patricio's voice carries over from the opposite end of the room. "One of the girls we rescued from that house the night we found your mother is a Russian mafia princess. The sister of Kostya Pashokov. He is the head of the New York bratva. She was kidnapped, and he is still concerned for her safety." *Fuck, I hope this isn't another offer for a wife.*

"She is going to stay with Adriana in California, and in exchange, Kostya wants us to take over his gun operation."

"Who was running it before?" Conejo asks.

"They were working with Los Hermanos Bandoleros, but Kostya thinks they may have been behind his sister's kidnapping."

"This will create us a new enemy with Los Hermanos Bandoleros," Conejo says, and I nod.

"Just let me know what you're going to need from me when the time comes," I say and move to the door. I've had enough of this shit for today. They could work on the details of this without me. I'm just here to collect money and to murder motherfuckers. My main focus right now is figuring out what Constance is up to.

I walk out the front door and light up a cigarette. I don't feel like walking to the Cuadri, and who knows how long it will be until Ricky returns, so I make my way out and walk to the front of the property. I can see Don Vicente working in his garden.

The old man's house is simple compared to the luxuries

of Patricio's home. I come up behind him, and when I get closer, he pulls a pistol out from his boot and aims it at me.

"Woah!" I say and put my hands out in front of me.

"Adriano? Is that you?" His eyes narrow as he takes me in.

"Mijo, you can't sneak up on me like that. I'm old and my mind isn't as sharp. You were two seconds away from a bullet in between your eyes." He lowers the gun and secures it back in his boot.

He motions me inside, and I make my way into the house behind him. I notice all the pictures on the wall. All the people I'm likely related to. I follow him into the kitchen, where he pulls out two beers from the fridge and hands me one. More pictures cover his fridge. Most of these of a young girl, holding the ugliest dog I've ever seen. Don Vicente catches my expression and chuckles.

"That is your cousin, Ariella, when she was younger. That's her dog, Guapo." Guapo, my ass. The dog is missing spots of hair, and the hair it does have looks mangled. He laughs at my expressions.

"She was thirteen when her parents found him on an abandoned property out in the mountains. There was a fire, and the people and animals had been burned alive, but somehow, Guapo survived. And your Tio Yeyo couldn't say no when she wanted to keep him," he says and shrugs as he takes a swig of his beer and moves towards the living room.

"This is her mother," he says, pointing at an older picture of a woman who resembles Olivia, but with darker features. In the picture, she's wearing a long gown and a crown with 'Texas' across the sash. Some type of beauty pageant she won. "You were named after her, you know?" he asks, but doesn't wait for my response. "Yes. She and your mother were good friends. Both beautiful and both troublemakers." He laughs.

"One time, I caught them stealing my 1964 Impala. I showed up at the party with Don Mario. He took out his pistol and started firing into the ceiling while letting out gritos. They were so embarrassed."

"Don Mario, the maintenance man?" I could imagine the old drunk screaming out and shooting up the place like an old Western movie. I didn't know he and Don Vicente were close.

"Ya... he was my right-hand man for a long time. And, well, no se quita el cabrón. He missed out on having his own life as a loyal hitman for me. He protected me and my family. I offered to buy him a house, but he wanted to live at the hotel. I know he pisses Enrique off, but I owe it to him. Plus, he still keeps me up to date with all the chisme." I laugh, thinking about the trouble the old man gets into every day.

"Here's Lola." He hands me a picture, and I expect to see another family member, but instead I see the '64 Impala.

"You named your car Lola?"

Don Vicente continues to fill me in on different stories about his prized car. He continues introducing me to every member of the family, including his late wife, my grandmother. I listen and take it in, laughing at his dramatics and jokes. A woman enters and makes us something to eat, and we settle down to eat off tv trays in the living room. It feels simple compared to the luxuries I've seen with other members of the Consuelo family.

The whole meal is spent watching game shows where Don Vicente yells, cusses, and verbally assaults every contestant. Homeboy don't play when it comes to Wheel of Fortune. Before I know it, time has flown by, and I hear a knock at the door. Ricky steps in, and I go to say goodbye. I stick out my hand, and Don Vicente grabs my hand and pulls me in, wrapping an arm around my shoulder.

"You know, mijo, Patricio is a stubborn son of a bitch, but he means well. He started building those houses ten years ago. One of them is for you."

Chapter Twenty-Four
Mireya

I woke up late and barely made it to class. Hence why my scrub pants are inside out, and I have two different black shoes. I sigh as I look down at the monstrosity. In my defense, I barely slept last night. I returned Adrian's truck to the hotel and grabbed a ride back home to the apartment with Alma. She was happy to have a night in, just the two of us, and I felt guilty for worrying about Adrian the whole night. I waited all night for a text or call, but it never came. I was trying not to act clingy, despite the nagging need to check on him. I tossed and turned all night, but nothing helped. My body was going through withdrawals from his touch. The warmth of his arms wrapped around me. The whispers in the dark. I was playing with fire, falling in love this quickly. I'd deal with the consequences after I got burnt. For now, I couldn't stop whatever this was between us.

I'm daydreaming about Adrian in the school library when I see a text come through.

> Alma: See you hoes tonight!

It's Thursday, but I haven't spoken to Thalia since she overheard what Bryan had said to me. We had both avoided the previous Thursday bar nights since then, but I could tell it was upsetting Alma. I had told her about our argument, and she was ready to be the mediator to help us get through it. She was depending on us coming together tonight, so I heart the comment. Not a direct no, but also not a yes. I would see how I felt later. I wanted to give Thalia the space she needed before tackling that conversation. Having tequila involved didn't seem like the best idea.

Something about today feels heavier than most days. I'm not sure if it's the lack of sleep or something with the moon placements, but I just wanted to go home and crawl into my bed and isolate from the world. These episodes were common for me. I could never pinpoint what triggered the feelings when they came up. Over time, I just saw it as my depression stopping by to hang out with my anxiety. I'd waste away in my room until Alma would pull me out of it.

I hadn't felt this way during the last few weeks, spending time with Adrian. I feel like I belong with him. And I never feel I belong anywhere. I don't have any real friends at school. Other than my friendships with Thalia and Alma, I keep to myself. Too many false scenarios play out in my head when I try interacting with other people. The toxic thoughts that they would eventually see me the way my mother did–stupid, ugly, and useless.

Adrian never made me feel that way. It was more than just the sex with him. Adrian is so rough when it comes to sex, but afterward, he wraps his arms around me, and I let that peace consume me. I know he worries about his darkness consuming me, but all I feel are his shadows protecting me, when everything else feels like it's falling apart around me.

The one thing making my relationship with Adrian difficult is my mother. I am convinced she was involved with what happened to Soledad after Adrian told me she was seen last with my mother. While she had always been the villain in my story, I never imagined she had played that role in the lives of others. Was she truly capable of such destruction?

After my last class of the day, I decide to confront the

matter altogether. I was already on a self-destructive path today, so why not go all the way in and stop by my mother's house? Misery loves company and whatnot. When I pull up, I notice an unfamiliar car outside her house. I circle around and park further down, hoping to get a look at her new fuck buddy.

I get in my backseat and grab a bag of hot Cheetos. I'm going to need a little snack while I start my own little Sancho stake out. These little meet ups never lasted long with my mother. She was too much of a bitch for any guy to take seriously or want something further than what she offered in the bedroom.

Alma has been texting me all day to make sure I will be there for Top Shelf Thursday. As much as I would rather go home and hide from the world, I can't do that to her. I have spent weeks ditching her for dick. Even if it is very good dick. As if I had summoned that very dick, I see a new text notification come through from Adrian. I am responding to Alma when I hear a door open and my mother's voice. I crouch down so they can't see me. If my mother comes out with her visitor, she will recognize my car and use it as an opportunity to embarrass me in some way.

However, to my surprise, it's not a man that walks out. It's Diana. She is wearing a black tank top, red high-waisted wide-leg trousers, and some white heels. My mother doesn't leave the door, but I hear her goodbyes and laughter. I sit up to get a better look. To make sure I'm seeing things clearly. Diana gets into her car and drives off. It was definitely her, but the question is how did she and my mother even know each other?

I'm waiting for Alma in the hotel bar. I figure I'll get a head start tonight, since I'm still trying to process what Diana was doing at my mom's house. I'm still in my scrubs and the two different shoes. I didn't have time to go home and change. Alma spots me; her eyes narrow and her brows draw together as she walks toward me.

"Well, Thalia is not coming," she says, rolling her eyes. She sees the top shelf in front of me and puts down her purse.

"I could have told you that."

"You two are really going to have to talk at some point."

"I know." I frown. "I don't know what's going on with me right now, to be honest."

"Well, it's pretty obvious you are getting good dick, and who am I to get in your way? I'm happy for you." She smiles at me and then orders herself a drink. Neither of us are big drinkers. With our matching sets of manic depression and anxiety, drinking really isn't in our best interest. We only really do this for Thalia, but tonight, I need something to take the edge off.

Alma starts talking about her newest book series and fills me in on three weeks' worth of maid drama. I look down at my phone to see the three missed calls from Adrian. I forgot to message him back after the whole failed Sancho stake out. Alma notices my change in mood.

"Is everything okay?"

I'm already three margaritas in, and I debate how far I'm about to go to explain that no, I am not okay. Not even a little bit.

"My life is fucked up," I start, and then it's really down the rabbit hole after that. Alma is concerned. I never really let her see this side of me, but I don't know where I fit in the world anymore. Things have been good with Adrian, but I know it's going to end, eventually. Once he finds out my mom has something to do with Diana, he is going to trust me less than he already does. Maybe Thalia was right. Maybe I need to end this.

"I don't know what's wrong, because I don't even know who I am if I'm being honest. I'm doing life on autopilot. You and Thalia stand out as individuals, but I am whoever I am around. Whoever I'm trying to convince to love me.

I do well in school so I can be the good student. I pour myself into work so I can be the reliable employee. I am the good friend, the good daughter, the good whatever the fuck I am to Adrian. It's exhausting."

Since Adrian has come back, I feel like a small part of myself is ready to submerge, to figure out who I am, because he was my missing piece all along. I'm so tired of always avoiding conflict and settling so others can get their happiness. I don't want to ruin whatever we are rebuilding here by just being whoever Adrian needs me to be.

"I want to find me, and just be me," I whisper, and Alma moves to grab my hand.

"And you will. Believe me, babe, I get it. You and Thalia are so brave, and I often feel like the weak one of the bunch. I mean, I cry at almost every Disney movie, for fuck's sake. But you are hardworking, not because you owe it to others, but I think deep down, you owe it to yourself. That is who you are. You never let anything hold you past the point of drowning. You kick, scream, and claw your way out. You fight for what you love, and I am grateful to have you as my friend."

I take in every word. I know we all battle different demons in our heads. A battlefield only we know how to defend ourselves against, but she is right about one thing: when I want something, I don't give up without a fight, and I want Adrian. I wanted him as a teenager, I longed for him throughout the years I went without him, and now that I have him, I will be damned if I let my toxic ass thoughts stand between us.

Alma is still smiling at me, and I'm tired of being this sad girl. The bar is starting to get busy, since it's Noche de Reggaeton, and the dance floor is packed. I grab Alma and we dance to Ando by Jere Klein. Our hips sway, both of us letting the music hit us and releasing the problems of the day.

With summer quickly approaching, the hotel is booking out every weekend. The closer the end of April draws near, more and more people will flow in and out of the hotel in preparation for Cinco de Mayo. Cinco de Mayo is a big event here because it is also Don Vicente's birthday. It is the second biggest event the hotel has, after the Dia De Los Muertos festival.

I smile at Alma, remembering that the entire Consuelo family will be flying in on their private jet. Screaming over the music, I say, "You ready to see Axel?"

Her eyes go wide and her cheeks flush. Axel Consuelo is Adrian and Thalia's older cousin. He has an identical twin, Adan, but their personalities are worlds apart. Axel is the playboy, while Adan is the tech nerd. Alma has had a crush on him since the first day she saw him. He even danced with her one time, and I'm pretty sure she had a wedding board on Pinterest the next day. I knew she was holding on to seeing him again.

"Ya." Her face lights up for a minute before her mood shifts.

"As long as Adrian isn't still cock-blocking me."

"I still don't understand your whole relationship with his friend Efren?"

"That makes two of us, then," she says, walking to the bar. I follow her, and she orders two shots.

"I got it," we hear a familiar voice say and look over to see Osiel. Osiel always has a playful smile on his face. I have spent more time around him recently, since he and Adrian work together. He's one of few Mexican men I knew with piercing blue eyes. It wasn't uncommon to have lighter features in our culture, but he did stand out. We shrug, and Osiel orders one more round of drinks for the three of us.

Arriba, abajo, al centro, y pa' dentro.

Chapter Twenty-Five

Adrian

I'm with Thalia and Ricky, picking up the twenty percent protection payments from different businesses around Houston. Thalia deals with most of the talking, while Ricky and I are just here for backup.

We're heading toward a nearby bank when we notice a group on motorcycles coming towards us.

"Who the fuck are they?" Ricky says.

"Oh, shit. Those are Los Bandoleros," Thalia says.

Before we can process what's happening, a shot fires in the distance, and the windshield shatters in front of us. Ricky swerves, and I move to check on Thalia.

"I'm okay. Keep driving," she yells, as she pulls an AK-47 from under the seat. Ricky floors it to get past them, and I start firing out the window. I hit one biker in the shoulder and watch as the motorcycle slides across the road. Others crash into him, buying us time. The back window shatters, and Thalia ducks before firing. They slow down, and Ricky continues speeding through traffic until they are out of sight.

"What the fuck was that?!" Ricky shouts.

"Go to Patricio's. I have a bad feeling this is about the Russians terminating their gun trade." Conejo had warned us it would start a war. I look back at Thalia. She's breathing heavily, but other than that, I don't see any serious injuries.

"No one thought to tell me that Los Bandoleros were our new enemies?"

"I just found out yesterday. One of the girls we rescued that night was the sister of a Pakhan from the New York bratva."

"I could have fucking died right now. It would have been nice to at least be briefed about having a target on my back! I saw a motorcycle tailgating us over an hour ago while you pendejos were arguing about which hot sauce was better. Had I fucking known, I would have said something. He parked outside Milagros Cocina, and I thought I was being paranoid. Pull over right now! We need to make sure he didn't put a tracker on the van."

We pull over and inspect the van. Just as she suspected, a tracker had been placed under the bumper. Had it been a bomb, we would have blown up. Anger flashes through me. Los Bandoleros wasted no time letting us know they wanted war. Gun trafficking was the most profitable resource for them. They wouldn't be willing to let go of their connection so easily. When we get to Patricio's, Thalia is still on one, cussing at everyone and demanding answers.

"You don't just take deals without consulting us," she says, pointing between herself and me. I honestly didn't think shit of it, but I see where she's coming from. I already have a lot of shit going on, trying to figure out what Bryan and Constance are up to. Now, we have to worry about going to war with Los Bandoleros.

Patricio is doing a great job of ignoring Thalia while she continues to go off. When she's angry, *olvidalo*. She shoots out verbal assaults like bullets from that AK-47. I'm sure she's insulted his manhood twice already now. She's pacing around the office like I do when I'm pissed off, hand on her head as her heels click on the floor beneath her. Patricio takes in her last insult before his own anger rises in response.

"You know what, chiquada? Get the fuck out of my office. Cool down, and when you're ready to talk like a big girl, you come back." Patricio leaves the room, and Thalia goes to follow him when I grab her.

"¡Ya dejalo! We need to just wait it out. Patricio has this

figured out."

"Does he?" Her tone is short. She's already willing to fight everyone she feels is a threat to her safety.

"I think he does, and while I appreciate you looking out for me, we need to make one thing clear: you do not speak for me. You do not dictate what I'm willing to risk and who I'm willing to risk anything with." She pulls back, and I know she understands what I mean–*who* I mean. I let what she said to Mireya go because I don't want to be in the middle of female drama. They can resolve that shit without me in the middle. But what I don't want is Thalia feeling like she owes me a life of butterflies and rainbows when that's never been reality for me.

She looks hurt, but follows me back to the van. Ricky stays back at the compound, so it's just me and her for the next hour. The first twenty-five minutes drag on as we sit in complete silence. When she finally breaks the silence her voice is calm and collected.

"We don't have regular lives, Adrian. We have a piece-of-shit father, and whether we like it or not, his ruthless blood runs through us.

"I know you said yes to this life, but I also know it was your only option. I just am not sure Mireya is cut out for it." She wipes her eyes as she looks out the window. "I don't want to be him."

I know who she means. She doesn't want to turn into our father. There have been a few times I've felt like that, too. I see it in Patricio's eyes, in my mother's eyes. The fear that I will become a ruthless monster.

"I would never hurt her. And to be honest, I'm getting sick of everyone thinking I'm not good enough for her."

She sits up straighter and looks at me.

"I never meant that, Adrian."

"No, but I know what you mean. You and I have had to harden our hearts to survive the life that was forced on us. I can't help but worry that I've already become him. But she keeps me grounded, she keeps me whole. I don't deny I am a monster, because I am. Mireya sees that monster in me, and she doesn't fear it. She hugs me and confides in me, like the fucking pendeja from Monsters, Inc."

"The monster from Monsters, Inc.?" She burst out laughing at the thought.

"Ya, bitch with pigtails and the big blue motherfucker." Luca had watched the same show over and over again, so I knew she understood the Pixar reference. When the laughing dies down, her expression returns to a serious one.

"I'm sorry, Adrian. I didn't understand how real this was to you, and I shouldn't have interfered or said any-thing. When I see Mireya, I'll talk with her."

"Thank you."

"I am still your big sister by six months, so I am not going to stop trying to protect you, but I will not interfere anymore. Te lo juro." She sticks out her pinky, and just like that, I've let my sister take away my manhood for a moment as I make her a pinky promise.

Chapter Twenty-Six

Adrian

Mireya hadn't answered me back about coming to the apartment earlier. Before we ran into Los Bandoleros, I had texted her, but there was still no response. I'm not far from the hotel when a message comes in from Osiel. It's a picture of Mireya and Alma laughing at a table with a group of his construction workers. Thalia has her feet up on the dashboard, filing her nails, when she looks down to see the photo on my screen. Her eyes go wide.

"Oh, shit."

'Oh, shit' is right. I speed up and pull in the back and make my way straight to the bar. Thalia is hot on my heels. I can hear the music as I get closer. If I get there and *my* ass is grinding on some other guy, I will pull out my gun and blast him. I'm relieved to see her sitting at the table when I reach the bar. Thalia is at my side now as we approach the table. I grab Mireya by the arm and pull her up. Thalia pulls Alma out of Osiel's lap .

"What the fuck!" Mireya says and tries to pull away from me, but I just grab on tighter.

"You two are drunk as fuck," Thalia growls, walking with Alma behind us towards the elevator. Mireya yanks free from me, and she and Thalia start arguing over Alma. I pull Mireya away, but she is persistent in confronting Thalia. Her words come out in slurs, but they flow all the same.

"You are not the boss of us! You don't dictate our lives!"

Thalia's expression mirrors mine as Mireya continues her protest. Heartlessness must be genetic. She ignores her and helps Alma, who is seconds away from vomiting in the corner.

"Mrs. Perfect here with all her secrets." I push Mireya into the elevator, and we ride up to the thirteenth floor.

"You were pregnant and never told us!" she blurts out. Thalia's eyes snap up. Hurt floods them. Her eyes meet mine, and she moves toward Mireya.

"Fuck you!" her voice cracks. The elevator doors open, and she takes off with Alma without a single look back. I sigh as I look down at Mireya. So much for everyone getting along. Mireya is processing the words she shot out. She's not completely belligerent, but she's far from sober.

She stands in the elevator, not willing to move.

"Get out."

"Machismo has been out since the 2000s, Adrian." I smile at her attempt at an insult.

"Have it your way." I throw her over my shoulder and she hits at my back. I slap her ass hard and walk into the apartment, then out to the pool. When I throw her in, she screams. The water isn't cold, but she wasn't expecting me to throw her in. She comes up to the surface panting. Her makeup runs down her face, and her scrubs cling to her body.

"Calm the fuck down." I pull up a chair and light a cigarette as I watch her make her way out of the pool. I'm not sure why she's acting like this. Brattiness is beneath her, but something must have triggered her emotions. She only acts this defiant with me when she wants me to dominate her, needing a release.

What I am concerned about is the way she is treating her closest friend. Despite their disagreement, airing out Thalia's dirty laundry like that was out of character for her. I watch as she swims to the pool stairs. Her teeth chatter, and I can see her hard nipples beneath the wet fabric. I put out my cigarette and walk away to give her time to sober up. I make my way to the kitchen to pour myself a drink.

I'm not in there five minutes before I hear her come inside, ready to pick another fight. Before she has the chance, I wrap a hand around her throat.

"Here's the plan–you are going to strip out of these wet clothes and get down on your knees like a good girl. You want to keep running your mouth? Then let me help you keep it shut." I slam her back into the wall. Tears gather in her eyes.

"What you're not going to do is self-destruct, get white girl wasted, entertain all of Osiel's co-workers, and ruin every supportive relationship you have. You're not going to avoid talking like a grown woman about whatever is bothering you." Her eyes bulge and she fights against my grip. I loosen my hold on her as she glares at me.

"Strip. Now." I remove my hand and she strips down, her body wet from the water. She watches me intently as she removes her clothing.

"Get on your fucking knees."

She drops to her knees, her lips parting slightly. I pull my hard cock out and stroke it a few times before I nudge her lips open. She takes me in, and I don't waste a second before I thrust all the way in. She gags when I hit the back of her throat.

"Goddamn. You're such a good little slut."

She moans around my cock, and I pull tighter on her hair. I continue to thrust into her harder as I listen to the gurgle of saliva. She sucks harder and uses her hand to gain better control. I watch as her other hand moves toward her pussy.

"Keep your hands off my pussy," I growl, and she whimpers, but quickly lets her hand drop to her side.

She thinks she's getting something in return by the way she's sucking my dick. She looks up at me, and the sight alone is enough to make me lose it. She swirls her tongue around my crown, and I pick up my pace, pounding into her mouth while I hold on to her hair in my fist. She moves her hands to my balls and squeezes them lightly. I lose all control as the sensation builds in me. My balls tighten, and I pull out just in time to paint her face. She's gasping on her knees, while her watered down mascara mixes with drool and cum leaking out her mouth.

"This is only the beginning of your punishment."

I pick her up and walk to the bedroom. I throw her on the bed and watch as her tongue slips out to the corner of her mouth, desperate to taste my cum. I spread her legs and her head falls back. She thinks this is it, that I'm going to return the favor. I grab the ropes from my closet and tie her hands to the bedpost. I go to tie her ankles, when I notice her white toenails.

When did she do that? My dick hardens in my pants at the sight. I never understood the hype about white toenails, but seeing the polish on Mireya does something to me. A hidden kink I needed to explore. I move to kiss her inner ankle and watch as her stomach sinks in. I run my tongue up the arch of her heel, and she moans in response. I suck on her toes, and she pulls on the restraints. I run a hand down her inner thigh before I reach her swollen clit. Her body trembles as my thumb circles her clit. I pull my hand back and slap her bare pussy. She cries out at the pain.

I bite her inner thigh, and she sucks in a breath. *A fucking goddess.* Her body is perfection. I slip two fingers into her and drop my mouth to taste her.

"I'm going to eat this sweet cunt the way you like it." I feast on her like a madman. My fingers dig into her ass cheeks. I gather the drool and cum leaking out of her with my middle finger. Coating her with it as I move to her back hole. I push a finger into the tight hole and bite down on her clit.

"Cum all over my face, mija. Your ass is taking my fingers so good." She starts to buck her hips, begging for her release. I take her right to the edge before I stop. I pull my finger out of her tight ass and stand to my feet as I wipe her arousal off my face.

"Adrian!" Her eyes shoot to mine.

I tie her ankles together and pull at the restraints. She looks ready for a crucifixion. My personal sacrifice. She's thrown off by my actions, but she'll figure it out soon enough. I had to pull back, despite wanting her to cum all over my face. This is her punishment.

"Goodnight," I say and kiss her on the cheek before I walk out the door. Leaving her unsatisfied as she calls me every name in the book behind the door.

Chapter Twenty-Seven
Mireya

When I wake up, my arms are sore. I had drank more than I normally do, but not to the point that I could forget the events that took place. The shit I said to Thalia. Adrian freed my hands last night after I passed out. I was pissed and horny all night. I tried to grind my pussy on a pillow to see if I could get some relief, but my body was too exhausted. I look down at my body and sigh. I need to get up to change these sheets and wash his cum off my face.

I make my way into the bathroom and take in the smell of him. I open his body wash and breathe it in. I could orgasm just at the smell. I turn on the water and scrub my body with the soap. I watch as my sweat, mixed with his cum, swirls down the drain. "Bye bye, babies," I say and laugh to myself. *Babies.* "Shit." It's then that I realize these little stay overs with Adrian have meant constantly forgetting to take my birth control pills every night. I've missed more than a few days. I should tell him to start wearing condoms until I can get back to a consistent schedule. He didn't cum in me last night, so I could just start today.

I step out of the shower and grab a towel. It smells like him, too. Fuck. I can't have a baby right now. *A baby. Fuck.* Memories of the shit I said to Thalia taunt me. I don't know why I even said that. Subconsciously, when Alma told me, I was worried about Thalia. I took that worry and turned it on her without even knowing the validity of the situation. She looked hurt, though, so I know there's something to this, and I need to get my mind together before I talk to her about it. I can't avoid conflict. Adrian has taught me that.

I reach into his closet and grab one of the black and white flannels off the hanger and put it on. I throw my wet scrubs in the washer, so I have something to wear when I leave. I listen for Adrian, but I don't hear anything in the penthouse. When I step out onto the patio, he is there, working out. He's shirtless. The sweat glistens off his back. I watch as he completes each rep, pushing his chest up and down off the concrete, unable to pull my focus away from him.

He notices me drooling over him and stands up. He smiles at me as he uses his shirt to wipe the sweat off his forehead. I'm leaning, with my arms crossed, on the sliding door. He makes his way toward me and pulls at the fabric of the borrowed shirt, kissing me briefly. "You look good in this." My cheeks flush at the compliment, and my stomach makes its needs apparent with a growl.

"Always hungry." He flashes me one of his rare smiles that I love so much. He grabs my hand and leads me to the kitchen. I could do more mornings like this, I think as I watch a shirtless Adrian make us breakfast. I scroll through my phone, and my chest tightens as I see the newest post on Alma's Instagram.

"This bitch knows how to cure a hangover," the caption underneath a picture of Thalia in a black-and-white striped shirt, a black beret, and batwing sunglasses reads. She holds a mimosa out, that lightly touches the glass at the end of Alma's hand. I frown and can't help but feel jealous I'm not there with them. Adrian serves me a plate, glancing at my phone briefly.

"Do you want to talk about it?" His eyes search mine.

"Is this how you get information out of me?" My brow arches. "Fuck me, feed me, and then I spill my guts?" He smirks, but I know he won't let me off easy. Adrian will push me to own my shit.

"I'm going to give her some space right now. I feel like shit, and I don't even remember everything I said, but I remember the basis of it. I know I hurt her."

"What happened yesterday?" He arches his eyebrow, and I watch as he eats a slice of bacon. Anything this man does is a kink of mine. Working out, licking mayo, eating bacon, I was turned on by all of it. He could get stuck in an inner-tube wearing flippers, like I did last summer at the water park, and I would still find it sexy as hell. I laugh at the thought and he looks up at me. Right, we were being serious. I push the images away for another day.

"I had a bad day yesterday," I tell him everything, from the two different shoes to the failed Sancho stake out. When I get to the part about Diana, he doesn't look nearly as surprised as I would expect him to be.

"Why are you not surprised?" He takes a drink of his coffee and sets his fork down.

"Yesterday, Patricio showed me some footage of one of my mom's hypnotherapy sessions. My mother was trying to confront her first association with the drug, and she mentioned your mother." He reads my scrunched up facial expression. My mother was a lot of things, but never an addict.

"I know your mother wasn't an addict, but something is off. Just a few weeks ago, Enrique showed me a video of her talking to someone outside the hotel, letting them know I had been released."

"Do you think she was talking to Diana?" I worry about what the two of them could have in common, feeling panic rising from my core. I wasn't sure if my mother had a part in Soledad's kidnapping, and I knew she was cold-hearted, but could she really be capable of this? What would her motive be?

"I don't know, but your mother has always hated me. At one point, while we were dating, she came over just to tell me I was a piece of shit who was holding you back."

"Is that why you broke up with me?"

"It was more than that. We were getting closer, and I knew I would eventually have to tell you about my mom. Then Constance planted her seeds in my head... Which is why I need to know if she was planting seeds in my mom's head, as well. Then figure out why." My throat feels tight. I didn't know she had said that to him.

"You can't tell her about this, Mireya. I'm trusting you to let me figure this out first."

"I would never do something to hurt you, Adrian. She is still my mother, though, and I want to be a part of any plans you have with her before you execute them." A part of me wants to believe she had no choice in this. Wants to place the blame on someone else and hopes there is a sliver of humanity left in her. Adrian is looking at me, and I know he can see through every worry and every wound surfacing. I get up and make my way to the couch. I push down the lump in my throat. *You look so ugly when you cry.*

Her words echo, and I continue to hold back the tears. After all these years, all these attempts to heal, I still have a hard time crying. It is a self-imposed punishment.

Adrian sits next to me and pulls me onto his lap. I hug him, needing an outlet. My heart is anchored to his, and when the toxic thoughts try to drown me, he pulls me out. I pull away and trace the outlines of his face.

"You don't believe her now, do you? That you don't deserve me," I whisper.

"Maybe she was right, maybe not. The difference between then and now is even if she is right, even if I'm not good enough for you, I don't care. You are mine." His eyes darken, and I wrap my legs so I'm straddling him and lean down to whisper in his ear.

"I've always been yours."

Chapter Twenty-Eight

Adrian

I've always been yours.

She has been, but to hear her say it–to whisper it ever so lightly in my ear–I want to burn the words into my soul. Her thighs open around my hips as she straddles me. In nothing but my flannel shirt, I can feel her bare pussy against me. She goes to break eye contact and move off me, but I grab her hips and hold them still. I hold her face to mine and press my lips to hers. I didn't let her get off last night, but the way she is rocking on my erection, I'm nothing but merciful right now.

"Does my little slut want to play?" I move her face and kiss under her ear, then lower on her neck. She grinds against my erection and moans.

"Look at you, so desperate for my cock."

She bites her lower lip and looks away again. I pinch her

nipple, and her eyes shoot back to mine.

"Look at me, and tell me what you want. Use your words." I let my hands slide under the fabric and stop on the side of her breast.

"I... I want you inside of me," she says, barely above a whisper.

"Pull my dick out of my pants." Her cheeks redden. She needs to own up to her desires. I know some men love a submissive woman so they can dominate them, but something about her taking control turns me on. I want her soft voice to speak dirty to me. I want her to break out of the lies in her head and own up to who she is and what she wants.

She's nervous as her fingers slip beneath my shorts. I let out a small laugh, and she scowls.

"Seriously? Sorry, I don't know what the hell I'm doing, Mr. Sex Expert."

"It's not going to bite you."

She rolls her eyes and I grab her by the neck.

"No seas chiquiada." I never was one to be turned on by a brat.

"Your pussy is leaking all over me. If you want me to make you cum, then I'm going to need to know what you want. Grab my dick and sit on it."

Her eyes feel with rage, but she pulls down my shorts

and removes my cock. She lifts herself, one hand on my shoulder for balance and the other guiding me into her. She feels so good. She adjusts to fit my length before she takes me in deeper. My own ecstasy. Satisfied with the pain, she moans.

"Eyes on me, diosa. I want to watch your face when I cum inside you."

"Don't stop, Adrian." My name rolls off her tongue like a prayer. Her hips grind against me.

"That's it, my little slut. Tell me what you want."

"Fuck me hard."

I unbutton her flannel slowly, button by button, until I see her breasts. Her brown nipples harden, and she arches her back, eager for my touch.

"Do you want me to make love to you like a goddess or fuck you like a slut?" I rub my knuckle over the peak of her left breast.

"Fuck me like a slut." The words a moan. I smile as I squeeze her nipples hard between my fingers.

"You like the pain?"

"Yes. I need more." Attagirl. I pinch her left nipple as I deliver a slap to the side of her right breast.

"Adrian." She gasps, her legs shake around me. "Oh... God."

I growl and pinch down on her right nipple and slap her

left breast. She goes wild as she bounces on my dick. I swim in the wetness gathered between her thighs.

"Good girl."

I run my tongue around the outer circle of her nipple, then suck it in sharply before I bite. She cries out at the pain. I remove my hands from her, and she stares back at me. After last night, she knows I'm capable of bringing her only to the edge.

"Keep going," she commands, and I smirk.

"Use your words."

"Suck on my tits. Suck them hard, bite me, scar me, punish me, claim me." It's the last thing I expect when she grabs me by the back of my neck and forces my mouth to her breasts.

"That's it, you little slut. Talk dirty to me." I return to biting her nipples as she bounces on my cock. Up and down. I reach back and grab her hair, forcing a bend in her back. I thrust from underneath as I hit a new angle, unlocking another level of pleasure.

Our bodies move in unison. I can hear her wetness as I thrust into her. The loud slapping sounds of our bodies is my new favorite song.

"Your dick is so big; I want you to rip me apart. I want to come all over your dick." Damn, this girl has a filthy mouth. I love that she is owning her sexual desires, reigning over them like the divine goddess she is. Nothing is as beautiful as the view in front of me. Sweat trickling down her neck. Her breasts bouncing with her movement. It makes me ravenous. It makes me want to be her God and her my equal. The only thing I bow to, the only thing I give into.

She's on the edge, and I slam my dick into her, filling her with my cum. She screams out my name, and I can feel the hot liquid as she squirts all over my dick. I can't help but laugh at the horror on her face.

"I... ugh... I'm so sorry. I think I peed on you," she says as she gets up to try to run to the bathroom. I hold her hips down on me.

"That's called squirting, and don't worry, I loved every second of it."

She collapses onto me, her forehead to mine. I pull her face to me and kiss her, feeling her knuckles brush the stubble of hair on the back of my head. Then the words that will damn us both fall from her lips.

"I love you."

Chapter Twenty-Nine

Mireya

I'm with Alma at Mr. Friborg's, her favorite Mexican Botanica. There's a large wall with natural medicines and herbal teas. My tia Vicky used to buy the Chupa Panza Tea, a pineapple, ginger, and flaxseed tea, that she swore was the natural equivalent of a BBL. My tia got real witchy when it came to her belief in herbal teas. But who am I to judge, since apparently, I am a squirter now. I spent thirty minutes googling the whole prospect of squirting, and I'm shocked that, as a nurse, I was unaware of this.

I scan over the different natural medicines. If only there was a tea here for bitches who say I love you too soon. If only I could go back and not have said that. My brain was in a trance from the orgasm and my emotions were high. Adrian had been kind enough to not make me feel any stupider than I already did after the words flew out.

He had kissed my forehead and carried me to the shower, where we cleaned up.

The sound of the door chime pulls me from my thoughts. Three young girls walk in and head straight to the candle section. Normally, I avoid coming here with Alma, because it creeps me out. Alma and Thalia love to have their cards read and dissect everything they were told together. When anything significant happens, they say, "This is exactly what Mr. Friborg said would happen." I don't want to know my future. My anxiety wouldn't allow for it. I have enough anxiety not knowing what the future holds, and my heart would shatter if I were told Adrian wouldn't be in it with me.

Alma, however, is in the back room getting her quarterly tarot reading while I scan the candle section.

Ven A Mi – to find love

Ven Dinero – to make money

I keep scanning until I see the candle I'm looking for. Santa Muerte. *Holy Death.* The female reaper matches the tattoo on Adrian's back. I want to take it to his house later. I noticed he had set up a small altar with her statue, flowers, and other offerings in the spare room.

"Does she call to you?" I jump at the voice, and turn to see Mr. Friborg behind me. The man is blindingly handsome. It's always hard to make eye contact with him.

"I... ugh... no, it's for my boy... it's for a friend."

"Hmmm. Well, might I suggest a bracelet then, for your friend?" He walks to grab a red stringed bracelet, and Alma looks at me and shrugs.

When he returns, he grabs my hand and slides the bracelet onto my wrist. Right above the gold bracelet Adrian had given me. He smiles at me, and I look down to examine it. It's a simple red string with a silver figure of the saint tied into the middle.

"For your friend, of course."

"Thanks," I whisper, and an odd chill slithers down my spine.

Alma and I leave after we pay for the items we grabbed. We catch up at our favorite taco truck, as we both avoid any conversation about Thalia. She tells me all about her card reading and how her true love is just around the corner. We walk around and visit the different shops. She stops in a local bookshop to pick up another fairy book to add to her collection. I find a small shop with Mexican household items and pick up a San Marcos blanket with a tiger on the front to take with me to Adrian's house. I noticed he doesn't have one, and no self-respecting Mexican man can survive long without one.

Alma and I both have checked out a bit.

"What's wrong?" I ask, pulling her attention back to

me.

"This week will be 10 years since she passed."

Alma rarely speaks about her mother, but she had passed away when Alma was thirteen. She had no other family and was put into foster care. She tried several times to do an ancestry DNA test to find her biological father, but every time, something would happen to her samples. They either got lost or destroyed in the mail. She gave up after the third try, trusting the universe did not want her to know him. Maybe it was for the best. I know Adrian and Thalia would much rather have never known their biological father.

"Mr. Friborg told me my father was close by. That when the moment was right, he would find me."

"You think he's here? In Houston?"

"I think I need to try another route. Maybe try and dig into my mom's past and figure out what I can. I already know she lied to me about a lot of her stories. My foster family couldn't even find any evidence of who she was when they adopted me."

It sounded weird, but I am the last person to question her mother's motives. Not when my own mother was plotting something.

"I'm going to ask Patricio to help me."

"Do you think he will?"

"Well, he just gave me a promotion and a long speech about being 'a hardworking woman who is representing the next generation of latina women,'" she mocks his voice, and I laugh with her.

"You got a promotion, amiga? Why didn't you tell me? I am so proud of you!" I reach over to grab her hand.

"It just happened the other day. You know Mr. Fri—"

"Ya. Ya. I know Mr. Friborg told you this would happen." She laughs before she grows serious.

"Why do you think he gave you that bracelet?"

"I don't know. Adrian is drawn to her."

"To La Santa Muerte?" she whispers, like she is afraid Death herself would appear like Beetlejuice if she said it too loud.

"Ya, he has a big tattoo of her on his back, and an altar in the penthouse."

"Who knew Adrian was so spiritual?"

"Maybe he gave it to me because I killed our relationship. I told Adrian I loved him after sex." My face falls into my hand. Alma's laughing so hard I think she might pass out.

"You did not. Please tell me this is a joke."

"I did."

"And did he say it back?"

"He literally just kissed my forehead."

"Oh, shit." She moves to comfort me.

"If you meant it, then don't feel bad. When we love someone, we shouldn't only express that when we are guaranteed they love us back. That's too safe. And boring. Love requires risks, and sometimes it's a risk not knowing how the other person feels."

She was right. I just need to figure out if the risk of loving him outweighs the pain I'd face if he isn't able to love me back.

When I get back to the penthouse, I decide to deep clean everything. Something about cleaning is relaxing to me. I place the candle I bought Adrian on his altar, next to another that is close to burning out. I move his laundry around, and then decide to relax and watch reruns of Vampire Diaries because my soul could use some Damien Salvatore. I can't be the only woman in love with an emotionally distant man. I fall asleep three episodes in, but wake when I hear my cell phone ringing.

It's my mother, and this is her third attempt. I still haven't had a chance to process what I saw the other day, and Adrian's confessions make me weary about what to say to her. I want to ignore it, like I usually do, but I need to get to the bottom of whatever she is plotting right now.

"Hi, Mom."

"Mireya. I haven't seen you in over two weeks! Have you forgotten about me?"

"No, I actually did go to see you the other day, but I decided not to go in, seeing as Diana was visiting you and all." I never speak to my mother this bluntly, and I can tell it throws her off when the line goes silent.

"What the hell was Diana doing there, Mom?"

"Excuse me? I don't have to explain who visits me, at *my house.* If you really must know, so you can sleep better at night, she came by to drop off an invitation for the engagement party."

"How do you even know her? And why would she want to invite her fiancé's ex-girlfriend's mother?"

"Oh, Mireya, don't be so dramatic." It's only a matter of time before she tries to gaslight me into making this about my own insecurities. Not today.

"You can stop with the bullshit. I know you're up to something, and whatever it is, just stop now before you get in over your head."

She huffs, and I can already hear the storm she's about to release.

"You know why Diana came over here? To warn me about your little thing going on with Adrian. He is still calling her nonstop. He is using you until he can get back to her, just like Bryan did." A verbal slap to my face. I feel the need to go back to my apartment as a panic attack rises in my chest. I grab my bag and head to the elevator. The phone still connected to the call, I try to block her out as I ride the elevator down. She's just lying. Just sticking her knife in.

"You are that pathetic that you actually believe he wants you?" The words start to echo around me. The elevator walls feel like they're caving in. She's pushing that knife in deeper.

"You are really as stupid as your father if you think anyone would love you." She pushes it through and slices me all the way open. This one takes me out.

I wake up in the elevator, hyperventilating. I must have fainted. I used to do that when I was younger. Stop breathing when I would try not to cry in front of my mom. Don Mario is in front of me, waving some kind of salt under my nose. Why the hell does he have that?

"There she is. What happened, girl?"

"I... I just feel like I'm going to—" and then I vomit all over.

Chapter Thirty

Adrian

I am in a good mood, the thought of Mireya screaming out my name still replaying in my head. The feel of her squirting all over me was the hottest thing I have ever experienced. I need to keep luring the freak inside her to come out and play. I bring my focus back to the empty table in front of me. This is not the time or fucking place to be thinking about my sex life.

I'm waiting for my mother. I'm hoping she is in a place that she may want to actually see me now. When she comes to the visiting area, I stand up to hug her. She squeezes me tightly and looks surprised I actually came to see her.

"Adrian. Mijo, what are you doing here?"

"I came to check in on you. How are you doing?"

"I'm doing good. I'm so happy to see you. I started hypnotherapy, and it has been helping me so much. I don't feel as many withdrawals."

"Ya, Patricio told me." More like he was invading her privacy and watching her sessions, but to-may-to, to-mah-to.

"Are you two getting along now?" Her face lights up, and her smile is so big that I don't want to disappoint her, so I nod.

"Patricio is a good man. I'm so happy he found you. I had hit the ultimate bottom of the barrel when they convicted you. I-I thought I had lost you forever—" she begins, and I wait to see what she has to say, but then she just stares blankly as she fights the tears.

The same way Mireya does. I know I crushed her when she confessed she loved me. I wanted to say it back, but I'm not sure. I'm not sure I can trust her, or anyone else, ever again. Especially when her mother has a vendetta against me.

Soledad grabs my hand from across the table.

"Where'd you go?" she says.

"Just thinking."

"I am here. If you want to talk about it. You've carried the world on your shoulders for so long, but I am still your mother, and I still love you."

"You don't think I'm a monster?"

"I think that neither of us were brought into a fair

world. You may have his blood, but you also have mine. I was lost, but when I find myself, Adrian, when I am able to show you a healed version of me, you will see yourself. You will see your strength and determination mirror mine. I may not have been the mother you needed, but I will make up for it." Her hand strokes my cheek. My chest aches at the words I've waited so long to hear. And just like I did with Mireya, I freeze up.

"Now, who is the girl?" she says, and my brows arch.

"A mother knows when her son is in love."

"It's Mireya." The words escape before I can think. I can't hide her from the world, and even if I can't admit what I feel for her, it doesn't take away from the fact that she's mine.

"Be careful with her mother, Adrian. Mireya has always loved you. I saw it in her eyes when she was a young girl, and I saw it again the night you rescued me. I don't think she ever stopped. Her mother is no better than your father, but she is not her mother, just as you are not your father. Just be careful."

"I don't think I can be the person she needs," I admit.

"Why not?"

"I'm not the flower-buying type. She has so much potential to be something in life, and I will just suffocate her."

"¿Y eso?" she scoffs. "Flowers die, mijo. Genuine love is

giving your heart to the other person." Her eyes warm.

"Is that how you feel about Patricio?" Her smile brightens at his name. Her love for him has survived through all the heartbreak and pain. Why couldn't mine with Mireya?

I play loteria with my mom and a few other residents until they are called away to dinner. I promise my mom to return within the next week before I leave. Taking out my phone to call Mireya, I see eight missed calls from Thalia. She doesn't pick up when I call her back, so I race back to the hotel. When I open the door to my penthouse, she is sitting in the living room.

"What the fuck are you doing here?"

"Oh, gee. My bad. Hi, Brother. Nice to fucking see you, too." My eyes narrow. "Ya. You're welcome. Mireya is in the back. Don Mario found her in the elevator. She passed out, and then she vomited everywhere. I brought her back up here, and she went straight to the room."

I push past her and go straight to the room while Thalia lets herself out. When I go in, I see her in the fetal position on the bed. She's staring out the floor-to-ceiling window that looks out over my balcony.

"Diosa, are you okay?" I cup her face and bring her into

me, sitting down on the mattress next to her. She finally lets out a sob, and I pull her closer to me. We stay like that for a long time, holding each other, until she has calmed down enough to look at me.

"My mom called me today."

"What did she say?"

"She said you were just using me to get back with Diana."

"Do you believe her?"

"I don't know."

"Is this because of what you said this morning?" She looks back out the window.

"I was thrown off by it, but it had nothing to do with Diana. I have only ever wanted you." She looks up and searches my eyes. Like she can detect the truth. I lay down beside her and run my hand through the long strands of her hair.

"I wasn't sure how to say it, or if it would come out right. I'm not romantic, and I sure as hell am not Prince Charming. I want you in a selfish way. It's toxic and possessive. I don't want to give into what I am feeling, but I don't want to lose you either. If we're going to do this, then I need to know that you are okay with my lifestyle and my choices. I pledged my loyalty to the cartel, and I can't trade your happiness for a lifestyle you may not want to be a part of."

"I love every part of you, Adrian. I would go to the gates of Hell themselves and offer my soul to have you. I don't understand everything you, or any of the Consuelos, do, but that has nothing to do with the way I feel for you."

I kiss her. *Kill or be killed.* I will kill every thought going forward that told me she deserves better. She deserves me, and I will make myself enough for her.

Chapter Thirty-One

Mireya

A week flies by as I prepare for final exams. I have all but moved into the penthouse with Adrian. We are lying on the couch, his legs around me as I lean back into him. His arm is draped over my chest, holding my hand, our fingers laced together. I convinced him to let me watch Vampire Diaries. He hates this show, even if, low-key, he knows he's the Mexican version of Damien.

"Do you think it's weird we found each other again after all these years?" I have convinced myself it was fate, finding him, but I'm not sure what he thinks about it.

"No. I think if two people are meant to be, they'll find their way back to each other." I feel his hot breath on me from behind when he speaks, his voice deep and raw, sending tingles throughout my body.

"I can still remember that first day you walked me home.

When those assholes were picking on me."

"Mmmhmm." His lips move to my neck. I suck in a breath as he kisses me there.

"Adrian! This is serious. Why did you stick up for me that day?" I turn to face him. There is this aching part of me that needs to know where this all started. Like the answer would be enough to understand how it would all end. He stares back at me with that familiar gaze, the darkness that drew me in.

"I saw those boys throwing rocks at you, and it pissed me off, so I did something about it."

"But you could have left it at that. Why did you keep walking me home after that?"

"Your dad paid me to." I gasp and move to leave when he pulls me back, so I'm sitting on his lap. He laughs as I pout.

"I'm just kidding, diosa. I kept walking you home because I wanted to figure you out. I always saw you as tempting and beautiful. After I beat the shit out of those boys, I thought you would run off. I thought you would be afraid of me like everyone else. But you smiled and thanked me, and that was the first time anyone made me feel worthy." His confession pulls me down deeper. That day he made me feel worthy, too. I had consistently dealt with kids poking fun at my weight, and he saw past it. I was surprised that anyone would stick up for me.

"But your dad did thank me for walking you home. I should have asked him to pay me." I playfully slap his arm and he laughs.

"What did he say?"

"He told me that no matter what anyone said about me, that he would always respect me for protecting you." I picture my father and a young Adrian. My father was a man of few words, but when he did speak, he was always direct and honest. Just like Adrian. He always challenged me to embrace who I was, despite my mother tearing me down.

"I miss him. I think I would be a more confident woman had he been around to raise me, instead of the insecurities I have now because of my mother."

"You can't let what she's done determine your self worth." He pulls me closer to him and kisses me softly. His lips are soft as he moves down to my ear and kisses me again.

"Did you like taking control the other night?" I lean back as he moves to my neck and collarbone, the delicate kisses a match to the parts of my soul only he could ignite.

"Yes." I hadn't fully taken control, but I had felt alive in the moment. It had turned me on to speak my desires. Suppressing them doesn't make sense to me anymore. Not when I am with someone so willing to give me the pleasure I crave.

"Tell me what you like, diosa, so I can worship you." My skin tingles at his breath on my ear. The words fireworks to my core. I'm in big trouble if this man's voice alone makes me wet. My vagina should be researched like Pavlov's dog, since apparently Adrian has conditioned it as well.

"Or would you rather I punish you?" His hands roam over my breasts—over the hard peaks forming—begging him to squeeze, suck, and bite them, desperate for him to mark them.

A loud bang at the door puts out the fire building in me. I jump up, and Adrian lets out a sigh as he walks to the door. I sit on the couch and wrap the San Marcos blanket over me.

"WHAT!" he yells as he fixes his erection and grabs his gun off the coffee table, and places it into his waistband.

"Adrian, open up." I recognize the voice. It's Thalia, her voice is frantic.

"What do you want, troll?" He looks out the peephole, unwilling to open the door. She keeps knocking until he opens it.

"Really, pendejo?" she starts, then her eyes catch sight of me. Thank the universe, Buddha, Jesus, and whoever else that I'm clothed right now, or else this would have been very awkward.

"We have to go to the compound; there's an emergency." A smile draws on her face when she looks at me again.

"Ewww, were you guys trying to get freak nasty under a San Marcos blanket?" My eyes shoot down to the fuzzy tiger blanket I am hiding under. I laugh at her playful tone and Adrian rolls his eyes. I know her well enough to know this is her extended olive branch. We'll talk about our problems in ten years. She doesn't do emotional stuff, and I have always respected her for that. It takes the pressure off both of us.

Adrian is already grabbing more of his guns from the armoire in his room and looking for his shoes.

"Do you have your medical kit? Some of the men are injured bad; they were attacked crossing the border."

"No," Adrian says.

"I'll grab my medical bag," I say and smile at her.

"No. I don't want you at the compound," he says again.

"Adrian, I've gone to the compound plenty of times before you," I say, hoping to ease his tension, but he only looks more annoyed. I look to Thalia for some help.

"She will be fine. We'll both be there to keep an eye on her," she reassures him.

Adrian sighs, but it's two against one.

It's times like these I wish I learned more Spanish. Sure, I can order a taco, sing karaoke, or understand a basic nursery rhyme, but trying to explain care procedures is way out of my comfort zone.

I'm working on setting up an IV for one of the gunned down men, while Gael removes a bullet from another. He's far from ugly, but I try not to look anymore than I need to with Adrian breathing down my neck. Thalia left with Conejo to figure out the source of the attack. Patricio is doing most of the translating for me, since Adrian refuses to be of any assistance. He stands with his lips tight and his nostrils flaring the entire time. I don't have the heart to tell him that, as a nurse, I will, in fact, be touching other men. I have a feeling he would start showing up at the hospital every day to monitor me.

The man I'm helping says something to me as I am cleaning up a wound on his leg. I look up to Patricio, but Adrian answers the man instead. The man's eyes go wide at whatever Adrian says, and I make out the apologies he offers. Patricio's expression stays neutral as he shakes his head, a small laugh trying to escape, but when I look at Adrian, there is no trace of humor on it. I look back down.

"He said you look like shit and smell like a wet dog. But don't worry, I told him that was rude, and he apologized immediately." A smirk is etched on his face.

I arch my brow, then roll my eyes, as I finish bandaging up the now nervous man.

Patricio lets out a laugh.

"Calm down, killer. We still have a few more men to go." Patricio pats Adrian's back, earning him a hostile glare.

We walk out of the room so I can give Gael my report.

"What did he say really, Adrian?" I say, crossing my arms.

He grabs me by the arm and slams me against the wall in the hallway.

"It doesn't matter what he said, because you belong to me and only me." I roll my eyes, and his hand reaches to my throat. "I don't like watching you touch other guys. I'd much rather watch them bleed out. I am trying to be merciful, but I am ready to go." He releases my throat.

"Why don't you go find Thalia and I'll finish up here. These men's lives are important. They are someone's uncle or brother. How would you feel if it was Patricio who was bleeding out when there was a nurse on hand to save him?"

"Please don't answer that," Patricio says, entering the hallway.

"Mireya, finish up, and Adrian, come with me to double

check the security of the estate."

Adrian narrows his eyes at me, and I watch as he silently debates his next move. I release a sigh of relief when he follows Patricio to the front door. I work in peace over the next hour, assisting Gael with a bullet wound and stitches. When Adrian returns, I pack up my bags and head down the stairs to the living room. Adrian is more on edge the longer we stay and wait for Thalia to return, so I suggest we walk down to Don Vicente's so he can relax.

"Adriano," the old man says from the porch, and I notice the smile on Adrian's face.

"Hola, Don Vicente." He takes me in and smiles.

"Mireya. Mireya, mija, is that you?" He looks to Adrian, and his smile broadens on his face. This man has always been so kind to me. As long as I've been friends with Thalia, he has treated me like one of his own grandchildren. Telling me family histories and giving me advice through his own personal life lessons. I adore him for that.

I walk up to the porch, but stop when Adrian grabs my hand. I freeze at the gesture. His hand is warm in mine. We usually stay at the penthouse, so I'm not sure if he wants to openly announce whatever we have going on. I'm not sure if it means to him what it means to me.

"Abuelo, this is my girlfriend." Butterflies fill me. I don't know who's happier in that moment. Me, for being introduced as his girlfriend, or Don Vicente, for being called Abuelo.

Chapter Thirty-Two

Adrian

Thalia is on edge when Patricio and I find her on the south end of the estate. She is ordering men to go through all the trucks to see if anything was taken or left behind. This is our first attempt at running guns for the Russians over the border, and we are certain it was Los Bandoleros who had ambushed us. There were motorcycle tire tracks at the site of the attack, and yet there were no guns taken. Patricio is convinced it was a scare tactic, but Thalia is shaken up nonetheless.

Mireya fell asleep as soon as we got in the car. Don Chente gave her some homemade moonshine, and they started talking about all the hotel chisme. I just watched them from afar while drinking a beer. I wasn't sure what had happened tonight, announcing her as my girlfriend. Maybe it was the possessiveness that consumed me while watching her work. I hated to see her touching a bunch of men. I knew most of them were horny sons of bitches. The way they looked at her. I wanted to slice their heads off. Part of me is set on making this woman switch professions when I marry her. But it's the marrying her part that's fucked with my head. I am envisioning forever with her, but I haven't even had time to figure out when these feelings surfaced or how to tell her about them.

I carry Mireya up from the car when we get to the hotel and put her in bed. We are all worn out from the night. I have a feeling Patricio is ready to declare war on Los Bandoleros, but we have to meet with the Russians first. I'm sorting through why they would leave behind the guns, while enjoying my 4AM snack, when I hear the sliding door open. I grab my gun and inch to the back, but stop when I see Mireya walking to the patio. *Naked.*

"Mireya," I say bluntly, as I walk toward her, but I can tell by her movement she is caught in her sleepwalking trance. I move to the front of her to block her way to the pool, her nipples hardened by the cool night's breeze. I slightly touch her, still afraid she'll punch me if I wake her up, but as soon as I touch her arm, she reaches out and grabs my dick. I stop and suck in a breath. Her grip is tight around me, and I can feel as my erection grows in her palm.

"Fuck me, Adrian," she whispers.

We've already talked about this, and at first, I thought the idea was creepy as hell, but I did some Google research on sexsomnia, and it's more common than I thought. Most people who have sexsomnia have to go to therapy with their partners because they were violating them in their sleep. I look down at her hand, where she's violating me right now, and I am too eager to let her; therapy the furthest thing from my mind. If her sex demons want to come out to play, then I'll let mine come out to join them.

She still has my dick in her left hand when her right one reaches to rub her nipples.

I gently remove my dick from her grip and move her to the nearest patio chair. She's compliant as she sits down on the reclining patio chair behind her. I run my hand over her face and trace the outline of her lips, my eyes fixated on the way the moonlight shines on her. *Una diosa.* I drop to my knees in front of her as my hands roam over her breasts and in between her thighs, memorizing every part of her.

"Adrian," she moans.

"No, mija, it's the Sandman, and I'm here to bring you a dream," I whisper into her ear.

I gently move her back on the chair and open her legs

wide before I glide myself between them. She locks her ankles around my back, and her back arches as I push in deeper. She moans the moment she feels the fullness of me inside her. In her semi-conscious state, she continues to repeat my name over and over again. I know she needs pain to fully release, so I suck in one of her nipples and bite down on it.

Her body jolts, and her eyes open wide. She takes in the view, her eyes flaring as she digs her nails into my back.

"Your sex demons wanted to play."

Her cheeks flush as she tries to regain consciousness. She knew we'd get into this position at some point. Judging by how wet she is, I know she's excited to be fulfilling her wildest fantasy. I readjust the chair so it's only slightly reclined. I don't give her time to fully adjust to her waking state before I flip her around, setting her on her knees.

"Grab the top of the chair."

She does as I say, pushing her ass toward me. I spread her ass cheeks and massage them gently before I slam into her tight pussy. I spank her hard, and she lets out a cry. I pick up my pace and spank her harder. Her ass is red as it bounces with each thrust. Her breathing accelerates as she rocks back and forth to meet my thrusts from behind. My thumb finds her clit, and I stroke around the swollen nub. She's panting, her hands clutching the top of the chair, but she moves into me. I rub my hand over her ass, and then I slap it one last time, as hard as I can.

She yelps and her pussy clenches on to me.

"Yes. Harder," she moans.

I pinch her clit. The chair squeaks with the pressure of our bodies slapping against each other. Her pussy is soaking and making its own sounds as I thrust into her. Her knuckles whiten around her grip at the top of the chair. I am not too sure the chair is going to hold much longer, but then again, neither am I. I pinch down on her clit again, and she lets out a loud scream. She squirts all over my dick, and I cum inside her, filling her up. I stay inside her as I savor every last bit of her orgasm. Then, all at once, the wooden patio chair breaks beneath us.

I grab her before she falls with it to the floor. We roll to the ground, breathless, as we chase our orgasms. We turn to look at each other and then back at the pieces of broken wood around us.

"Enrique's going to kill me."

I look to Mireya to make sure she's not hurt, but I'm met with her laughter as she looks back at me. I stand and help her up. Once she's on her feet, I throw her over my shoulder and spank her ass. "Let's see what other furniture we can break."

Chapter Thirty-Three

Thalia

Lucia is cuddled up next to me while Luca is sprawled out on the other side. I know he's awake. He barely sleeps with this little brain always going a hundred miles an hour. I hear a knock at the front door, but I'm hoping Olivia can get it because it's my top priority to isolate from the world today.

I've seen a lot of shit in my twenty-two years of life. Patricio has been preparing me to one day take his position running the finances of the company, as well as take on the Financial Networking of the Houston Cartel Connect. Making it in a male-dominated world has never been easy, but I've learned to separate my emotions from the violence I am surrounded by. I am numb to it. But yesterday was something personal, and not for Calavera Hotels, or even the Consuelo family, but it was a personal message for me.

Conejo saw it first and stuffed the note in his pocket. It was lying next to a massive pile of burning baby dolls on the border of Patricio's property. When he told me about it, I cringed at what the message could mean, but then I saw the note.

What did you do with the baby, Thalia?

A personal message and a direct threat. I needed to figure out where it came from. I needed to talk to my tio and let him know the attack very well could not have been Los Bandoleros, but rather, someone from my past. The knocking on the door becomes louder, and when I finally get up, I see my brother outside the door and narrow my eyes.

"¿Qué quieres güey?" He arches an eyebrow at me, clearly offended at my harsh greeting. He ignores my question as he pushes past me.

"Nice to see you, too. No time for a family breakfast?" His tone is playful but arrogant.

I walk to the kitchen and throw a Pop Tart at him.

"There, now get out." He rolls his eyes and Luca has already heard him and runs in to hug him. Adrian has already embraced Luca and all his weird quirks. La sangre llama, my grandmother used to say. The Spanish phrase about our bloodlines calling to one another has made more sense since Adrian showed up. Luca has little sense of social skills, and avoids most people he meets, disregarding their presence, yet, he followed and clung to Adrian from the moment he met him. The same way he did to Olivia, Lucia, and myself.

"What happened last night? You looked shaken up. Did you find something on the property?" He opens the package and hands one of the Pop Tarts to Luca.

I debate what and how much I should tell him. Maybe, had we actually grown up as siblings, this would be easier, but we are both fucked up estranged children of Ivan Consuelo.

"There was a threat," I finally confess. "A personal one. For me."

I tell him about the note and the display, wrapping my robe around myself as I sit down on the couch next to him. Feeling defeated about the whole thing and scared of letting him in on this detail of my life. I never know who I can trust, and therefore, I trust no one outside my family.

"I don't get it? Who would want to hurt you?" I close my eyes and brace my inner child to take cover so I can open up to Adrian.

"When I was sixteen, my–I mean, our–father arranged me into a marriage with the son of a Kingpin. He wanted to form an alliance with the Los Reyes de Tamaulipas, who, at the time, had control over Reynosa. Our entire family fought against it, but in the end, I was dragged to the altar."

My eyes wince at the memory of one of the most pivotal points in my life. "The day after we consummated the marriage, his entire family was arrested on charges of drug trafficking and money laundering." Adrian looks at me, confused, as he takes in the information.

"What happened to your... *husband*?"

"Ivan had betrayed the entire family, set them up, and even killed the ones who went to jail. He used Olivia's ex-boyfriend, who was an informant at the time, and brought them down at my wedding. He used the wedding to gather them all together. Those who were tried and arrested died after he bombed the bus that was transporting them. My... husband... was arrested alongside them. It grew into a messy war that took years to straighten out. For my safety, I was taken to California, to Tia Adriana's Ranch, where she has maximum security due to her husband's status. Aurelio, her husband, held rank with Los Reyes. He made a deal for my protection, and within a few years, our father's head was cut off and sent to Don Vicente."

"Then what changed?"

"I'm not sure. I couldn't see Los Reyes retaliating. Not with whatever deal they struck with Aurelio. They control their territory, and we rarely cross paths."

Another knock sounds at the door, and Adrian looks at me as I move to open it. Standing outside is my cousin Ariella, holding her demonic-looking dog, Guapo. Looking the very essence of a narco princess, dripped in a short brown designer dress, designer bag, and heels. Her lighter complexion is flawless and her green eyes are twinkling with mischief, as always. Adrian walks behind me to the door and gasps at the ugliness of Guapo and crosses himself before walking out. Ariella looks puzzled as he walks past her.

"Um. Rude!" she yells behind her. "You really pick them well, Thalia." I laugh at her confusion.

"That is actually Adrian, my brother," I say, and her mouth drops. Adrian has always been a whispered name in our family. Most of us were convinced he was a ghost who we would never see.

"I'm going to need all the tea!" she says, and I hope she has a few hours because I'm going to need it to explain everything.

Chapter Thirty-Four

Adrian

It should be illegal to own a dog that ugly. My grandfather's birthday party is still a month out, and family I have never met are flying in left and right. I am relieved when I reach Enrique's office to see he is alone. He had messaged me to meet him down here, and I'm assuming he's found more information on Constance.

"You look like you've seen La Llorona," he says when I walk in.

"More like a demonic dog."

"I take it you met Guapo, then," he laughs. "Your other cousins are parading around here. Adan was able to get me the phone records on Constance. It appears we were right: that call she made was to Bryan." I had already figured as much. I had more important things to figure out before questioning Bryan myself. With this new information

Thalia shared with me, I feel like there is a much larger threat hanging over us than whatever Constance and Bryan are scheming.

"There's more. Don Mario caught Bryan snooping around here, meeting one of the sous chefs after hours."

"Where's the sous chef?"

"Axel got in last night and was bored, so he asked if he could torture the poor soul. The guy confessed that Bryan was paying him to get samples of DNA. Your DNA, Mireya's DNA, and even Thalia's. I went back through the hotel security footage and found him collecting hair, a glass you had drank out of, and the sick fuck even had one of Thalia's tampons." I cringe at the desperate attempts.

"Why the hell would they want a DNA sample from each of us?"

"Por favor, Adrian. Crime and extortion is your job. Which is why I am giving you the information. Use your own methods to figure it out." He rolls his eyes and straightens the lapels of his jacket. "I'll call Axel in, and I'm sure the two of you can bond over torturing Bryan together."

I had been biding my time with Bryan, but he is becoming a bigger threat than I had suspected him to be. I'm not about to let him throw Mireya and Thalia into his plans. It looks like it's time Bryan and I have a little reunion of our own.

Turns out Axel is a psychopath. The moment I met him, I could tell he had one of those detached god complexes. He wore a designer suit with gold chains, rings, and a bracelet. Above his right eyebrow, he had tattooed the word DES-MADROSO. It fit, considering he seemed reckless and unhinged. Adan, his identical brother, opted for a calmer look. He wore casual joggers and a black hoodie. Where Axel was all brawn, Adan was all brains. A tech nerd whose father used his skills to hack into enemies' territories and dismantle high-end security systems. He was active in the cyber cartel and was able to expand profits with cryptocurrency. Finding a person's location was child's play to him. He located Bryan in less than an hour.

"So, what's the plan? Kill on sight?" Axel says as he kisses the gun he's carrying. We're in the operations van. Thalia joined us while Ariella watched the twins. She watches Axel and rolls her eyes at his antics.

"No, we need to be smart, figure out what the connection is, and keep him alive for questioning." She sounds just like Patricio.

"The only one allowed to kill him is me." I look directly

at Axel.

"Okay, bet. I like this guy, Adan. You could learn a thing from him." He elbows his brother, who keeps a straight face, avoiding his brother's commentary. I've learned that Adan doesn't talk unless necessary, and I appreciate that, considering Axel does enough talking for the both of them.

"He's not some guy. He is your cousin, cabrón," Thalia says, coming to my defense.

"Even better. Mas vale onza de sangre que libra de amistad," Axel replies, and for the sake of this operation, I hope that's true. Since getting out of jail, I've learned the only people I can depend on are my family. My blood. *My sangre.*

We drive up to the compound where the men are keeping Bryan. He's handcuffed to a metal post, and his face is already bloody from their attempts to get him here. He sees me and smirks.

"Long time no see, Adrian." He laughs. I fail to see the amusement, since we clearly have the upper hand here.

"What the fuck are you laughing about?"

He spits at me, and I grab him by the hair and drive my first into his face.

"Still jealous I took your bitch, I see."

"More like you just love all my leftovers."

"Bor-ing." Axel fakes a yawn and steps in, pointing a gun in his face.

"I have a week's worth of high-end Texas pussy waiting for me, so if we could hurry this little reunion up, I would appreciate it. Why were you gathering DNA samples?"

Bryan's eyes widen. When he refuses to answer, Axel cocks his gun and begins to count down.

"Three, two..." A shot fires into Bryan's left leg and he lets out a cry. I glare at Axel and he shrugs. Bryan's screams echo off the walls, and he lays down on the cold cement floor in the fetal position, unable to move his hands to the wound.

I crouch down, gun in my hands, and look at him.

"Why did you need our DNA? Were they for Constance? I know you're working for her."

He scoffs. "Constance is the least of your worries."

"Answer the fucking question."

I hear Thalia's heels click on the floor behind me as she walks forward. She walks to him and his breathing becomes shallow as he tries to breathe through the pain of the shot. She bends down and sticks her long nail into the bullet wound, and he screams, a satisfied smile appearing on her face.

"FUCK! Okay, okay. I'll tell you, just... just get me help. I don't want to die," he cries out, and she removes her finger nail.

"I got the samples for Claudia. She... she asked for them, but I don't know why."

We all look at one another, unsure who Claudia is.

"Who is Claudia?" I ask, when I notice none of us are familiar with the name.

"I... I don't really know. She came to me a few months ago. Julian has been blackmailing me since high school. He was the one who set you up and forced me into this fucking marriage. Claudia said she would get me out if I gave her information."

"What kind of information?"

"Just the DNA samples. Constance has been looking for a son she had. My guess is that Claudia is looking for him, too." He's sobbing as his leg continues to bleed out over the pavement. "I never wanted to be a part of this. I just don't want to marry that crazy bitch."

Son? Mireya never told me she had a brother. By the confused look Thalia has on her face, I'd say she knows nothing about this, either.

"He could be lying?" Her eyes narrow on him.

"I could be." He smiles. "But I don't give a fuck what you think. Julian and Constance have been looking for some fucking long-lost son of hers. That's the truth."

"But why would you need our DNA?" Thalia says out

loud, a question to herself. A puzzle she needs to solve.

"My guess is that the son is somehow related to the Consuelos. Julian and Constance didn't want Adrian finding out he was a Consuelo because that would make him the rightful heir of the company, being the oldest son of Ivan."

Thalia and I look at each other. Before Bryan can say another word, we hear a gunshot fire. The blow is delivered directly between Bryan's eyes, and he falls to the ground in front of us. We turn to see Axel.

"We got what we needed," he says. I glare at him as I watch the blood pour from Bryan's lifeless body. I still had questions, and now I was suspicious of why Axel was so quick in killing him. Adan sighs, and Thalia's face reflects mine. How about that for family bonding?

Chapter Thirty-Five

Mireya

I'm in my apartment bathroom, peeing over a pregnancy stick. No big deal. With final exams, work, and fucking Adrian, it turns out I forgot to take my birth control again. Don Cheetos barges through the door and looks at me.

"Stop judging me," I say to the cat and grab my phone to set a timer. I look through my text messages and laugh when I see Alma's text.

> **Alma: Why did no one tell me Axel's fine ass was in town?**

She sends a picture of Axel to the group chat she shares with Thalia and I. Axel is standing with Adrian outside the lobby elevator. I smile when I see Adrian. He's wearing brown Dickies pants, a white shirt, and all white shoes, the color complimenting his skin tone. He always had a laid back style, but it is the body I know is hidden beneath the clothing that makes my knees weak.

Thalia: Stalker

Thalia and I's relationship is still on the rocks. She took me to the compound the other night, and things seemed like they had a chance of going back to normal, but she has been quiet at work. Almost like she is avoiding me. Adrian says it has nothing to do with me and to give her time. My phone timer goes off, and I walk back into the bathroom to read the test. There is no 'yes' or 'no', just a little arrow pointing to a book. I pull out the instructions and try to figure out what it means. I'm sure it means something along the line of "stop having unprotected sex and study, puta." I laugh to myself, but then remember this is no laughing matter. I don't know if I'm ready for a kid right now. After reading over everything, I figure out the symbol means there was an error and I need to take another test. Thankfully, I bought the pack with two.

This is scarier than watching the Blair Witch before a camping trip. I go to down some ice-cold water. I can't have a baby with Adrian. I don't even know how he feels about me. I already told him I love him, and he did introduce me as his girlfriend, so obviously, he wants to be with me. I'm not sure it means forever, though. He has his ways of showing me he loves me, but I just don't know if it's like real, durable, have-my-babies-and-forever kind of love.

What I do know is that since he came back into my life, it's like I'm slowly finding myself. He's forcing me to speak up for myself and what I want, even outside the bedroom. When I'm not around him, I want to be, and when I am with him, I want the minutes to turn into hours. There is so much that I still don't know or understand about what Adrian does. About what any of the Consuelos really do for a living. I know they are involved with the cartel, and have pieced together the basic idea. I don't ask much because I know deep down I don't want to know all the details; I'd love him, regardless. Even when I thought our paths would forever be separated, the universe led us back to each other for a reason. I would hold on to that.

I finish folding the laundry, and go to take another test. I try the dipping method, since a girl on YouTube swears it to be the most effective way. My ass is still sore from the other night, so I rub some cream on it and smile at the thought. How he fulfilled my fantasy of fucking me in my sleepwalking state. I thought I would wake up scared and violent, like I did with the girls that one time, but when I awoke and saw it was him, the violent urges only sparked my arousal. It excited me. Like that moment before a rollercoaster drops, or jumping off the high dive into freezing cold water.

I hear a knock on the door and place the test on the sink as I go to answer it. When I open the door, I feel a sharp pain in my face. After being hit in the face, I stumble backward, and a black cloth bag is placed over my head. I try to fight against it, but I'm too late. I can't see anything, but I can hear voices. One I recognize well–my mother's. I plead through the bag for her to release me. I am going to suffocate in here.

"Stop crying, Mireya. You look ugly when you cry."

A male voice appears from the bathroom. "You might want to take a look at this."

I calm my breathing enough to focus on the voice; I don't recognize it. His footsteps draw near to me, and I can barely concentrate while my mother ties my hands together.

"It's a pregnancy test," the voice says. My mother squeezes the rope tighter.

"Nothing we can't take care of." A minute ago, I was unsure if I wanted a kid, but now I'm afraid I won't have a choice. And for once, I'm glad she covered my face as I silently let the tears fall, fear growing in the pit of my stomach as I imagine the lengths she'll go to punish me and my baby.

Chapter Thirty-Six

Adrian

I didn't have time to question Axel, and Bryan seemed a far less threat to us with Mireya missing. I pace Patricio's home office. It's been fourteen hours since I found out she was gone. Every emotion, from rage to worry, has surfaced since. My chest aches and my mind is slipping.

Eight hours ago, Alma messaged Thalia, worried about Mireya. We went straight to the apartment, and it had been destroyed. Thalia called Rocky, our cop on the inside, and he questioned all their neighbors, but no one had seen her. Four hours later, I received a text message from an anonymous number. It was a picture of Mireya, chained to a pole, her mascara running down her face, lying on the cement floor. I had zoomed in to try to pin a location, but only a cement wall could be seen behind her. Panic makes its way up my stomach, and I'm ready to kill whoever did this to her.

Adan traced the number back to Diana, but when we went to trace the location, it was a dupe. Instead of finding Diana, we found a box containing her phone, a pregnancy test, and a congratulations card.

"What the fuck does this mean?" I shove the box onto Patricio's desk. I haven't eaten or slept. Looking at Thalia, who is pacing around, I can tell she hasn't either. The image of her plays over and over in my mind. Enrique took Alma to his house and is watching her until we can figure out where Diana is keeping Mireya.

"Either Mireya is pregnant or this is another weird baby threat towards Thalia," Patricio says and frowns.

Thalia turns to face him. She tilts her head and narrows her swollen red eyes.

"What do you mean, *another* threat?" Her head turns quickly as she sends a hostile glare to me.

"I didn't say shit about what you told me." Whatever Patricio knows about the threat, it didn't come from me, and we both know Conejo is loyal to a fault.

"There have been some... unusual threats sent to the hotel recently. All addressed to you. Sometimes it's baby clothes, baby toys covered in blood, or distorted baby dolls. Doña Clara found each of them, and Enrique and I have disregarded them until we locate the source," Patricio explains.

"And you didn't think it was important I know about this?"

"How did you find out?" His eyes widen when she explains to him what she saw the night our men were ambushed at the border. The night we thought we were attacked by Los Hermanos Bandoleros. Patricio goes quiet for a moment. His hands nervously scratch at the back of his neck.

"It doesn't make sense. I don't know who would do this. We hadn't accepted the treaty with the Russians yet when we started receiving the threats, so it's not Los Bandoleros." He paces behind the desk. "Los Reyes wouldn't hurt you because you're Yeyo's niece; they accepted Ivan's death as payment, and they have nothing to gain from threatening our family."

"It has to be Constance, then. She's fucking with us," I say.

"The messages are too personal. What would Constance gain from torturing me?" Thalia asks.

"Ivan killed the majority of the Macias family who attended the wedding. We need to gather a list of everyone who knows about you, and..." Patricio stops and looks at me, debating whether he can trust me.

"And the baby," Thalia says as she looks at me. A confession. A secret she needs me to hear because she trusts me. Thalia trusts me because she knows I will protect her. The same way I would protect Mireya and go to war for her. Thalia is my blood, and she has proven to be my greatest confidante since I got out of prison. I nod in gratitude and watch as she swallows to hold down the tears. She turns from us and takes a moment. Before the silence consumes us, she rolls her shoulders back and readjusts herself so she is standing straight. When she faces us again, she has regained her composure. That unphased chingona look returns to calm her nerves, her badass alter ego that protects her from losing her footing in the male-dominated world she was thrown into.

"We need to find Mireya. Then we can figure out where the threats are coming from."

I agree. Mireya is my top priority. I can't let what happened to my mother happen to her. I can't let them hurt her anymore than they already have.

"I've reached out to our allies to see if any of them have worked with Julian or knew about Constance. None of them did."

Adan had hacked into Julian's computer as soon as we found out they took Mireya and found money wired to a private investigator several years ago. Axel and Adan took off to Matamoros last night, as soon as they found out

Mireya was missing, to find the man.

"What did they find out about the P.I.?"

"He was a member of Los Peregrinos Motorcycle Gang. He was providing Julian with false information to throw him off one of their members. It had nothing to do with you."

I pour a shot out from Patricio's bar and hand another glass to Thalia. Another dead end. I am trying to keep calm, but we are wasting time.

"We're lucky they didn't declare a war after Axel insulted them. After that, they were unwilling to cooperate."

I down my shot, and Thalia rubs at her temples.

"What about the Claudia bitch Bryan mentioned?" He had mentioned the name, but none of us knew who she was. She could be the person helping Diana and Constance. The one calling the shots and behind everything going on here. Patricio scratches at the back of his neck, taking in the information, when we hear a knock on his office door.

"Sir, there is a woman out front looking for you." Patricio's housekeeper stands in the doorway. The three of us look at each other and then make our way down the stairs. When we get to the staircase, we see a woman standing at the entrance. She appears to be in her late 40s, but she's clearly had work done to make her look that young. She's dressed in a short, fitted black dress with wide sleeves, long black lace gloves, and a black straw hat with a mesh panel. Sunglasses cover her eyes. She smiles when she sees us walking toward her.

"Buenos días, señora. How can I help you?" Patricio says as we move towards the woman.

"Buenos días. My name is Victoria Robles. Your nephews were turned away from Los Peregrinos last night. They were not impressed with how disrespectful the one with the face tattoo was." Her gloved finger runs across the top of her eyebrow. Like we would need a visual on Axel.

"However, had I known what the situation was, I would have convinced them to help. My apologies on their be-half, but I brought you something to make up for it." She points behind her, and Thalia looks at me hesitantly. She makes her way out the door, to her Bentley parked outside, and we follow. Thalia pulls the gun from her waistband, and I do the same. The woman, Victoria, pops open the trunk, and we all take a step back when we see what she has inside.

"I'm sure you are all well acquainted with my dear ex-sister-in-law, Constance Torres."

A terrified Constance stares at us as she fights against the restraints. The woman has her hog-tied, with duct tape covering her mouth.

"Now, you will lead us to Mireya, and in exchange, I will give you the information you seek about your son," Victoria's voice is polished, but also sounds like a villain from a Disney movie. Her smile is evil as she stares down at Constance. Constance fights the restraints and attempts to scream through the duct tape at the woman.

"You're... you're Mireya's aunt. Her tia Vicky," Thalia says, and I put it all together. I always pictured an older, soft woman who baked cookies and attended mass three times a week. I was not expecting a future version of Thalia, dripped in all black, with heels and a creepy smile. I'd question how she kidnapped and hog-tied Constance in seven-inch heels, but I've seen Thalia in action.

The woman removes the duct tape, and Constance begins a cycle of cursing and threatening, which fades to pleading and crying. The woman is unimpressed with her tears, as am I. She doesn't have any solid information we can use, since she was also blindfolded during the transport, but she gives us the name Julian had used when purchasing property to use for his gambling rings. Patricio runs inside to call Adan. Once he runs the fake name, we are able to locate a vacant automobile repair shop an hour away on the outskirts of town.

Only sixty minutes stand between her and I. I have been through every form of punishment during this life I have been given, but these sixty minutes would be the cruelest form of punishment I've ever experienced.

Chapter Thirty-Seven

Mireya

I'm breathing deeply, trying to not hyperventilate under the cloth bag around my head. I listen as the driver throws my mother in the back seat next to me.

"Get this bag off me!" she screams.

I can't see anything, but I can feel the commotion of a vehicle. She protests, and their arguing continues, before he throws her out of the vehicle. She's probably disappointed she won't have a hand in torturing me. When I hear the vehicle stop, I sit up. My door opens, and the hood is ripped off. Diana stands in front of me.

"Where the fuck is he?" she asks. I am not sure who she's talking about, and she punches me in the face when I don't answer quickly enough. I wince and pull on the ropes around my wrists. I kick her and she falls backward. Before I can take off, the man helping her grabs me and hauls me back *toward the building. A large rusty sign hangs above the garage. Primos Auto Repair. The shop is vacant, and I look around to see there are not any visible houses or stores nearby.*

Diana pulls herself up from the dirt.

"You fucking bitch. Where is Bryan?" I spit in her face. It's a final attempt to let this bitch know I'm not going down that easily. She grabs me by the hair.

"Miss. She's pregnant." The driver hands her my pregnancy test, and she smirks. I'm not sure if the revelation will help or hurt my attempts to break free from her.

"She's not pregnant in her face." Another blow, and this time, she uses all her force, hitting me a few more times before she is satisfied.

"Your baby daddy took Bryan, so until he returns him to me, you are collateral."

I'm floating in and out of consciousness; too tired to be fully awake, but too afraid to fall asleep. I had kicked and screamed while Diana and the man handcuffed me to the pole. My face hurts from the numerous blows I've taken. Diana had mocked me as she took pictures to send to Adrian.

When I open my eyes, I can tell it's nighttime. The building is dark and smells like gasoline. I take in my surroundings. There are several empty lifts above me, air compressors, and tires surrounding the back wall. I look to the garage doors and see the stars outside the dusty windows. I don't hear anything. No footsteps or voices. It's safe to assume I'm alone for now.

I struggle against my restraints, wanting to wrap my arms around my stomach, wanting to comfort the life inside me. My baby. *Adrian's baby.*

"Please," I cry out and slide with the handcuffs up from the concrete floor. I pull on them hard, trying with every last bit of my strength to yank myself free. I exhaust myself in my attempts and slide back down to the floor and bring my knees up.

"Please just be okay," I whisper to my unborn child. I hope Adrian finds me soon. Diana needs me alive if she plans to use me to get Bryan back, but I am not sure how long that will be. The toxic thoughts running through my head have me questioning if Adrian would even be willing to give up his revenge on Bryan in exchange for my life. I shut them down and focus on my breathing. I know from classes I took on Child Development that everything I feel, my baby can also feel.

My eyes look to the gold bracelet Adrian gave me, and to the red string bracelet with the metal Lady Reaper bead placed in the center.

"Please. Please, if you are willing, spare us this death," I cry out to the angel of death.

I cry myself into a restless sleep. Visions of Adrian, the lady reaper, my friends, and my unborn child appear in my dreams. At some point, I feel a warm sensation wrap around me, the sound of a distant lullaby. Maybe death has come for me, after all.

I wake in a panic when I hear gunshots outside. A vehicle drives straight through the garage, and immediately I see a figure jump out and run toward me. I close my eyes, unsure of who is coming at me. There is a fearful part of me that worries Adrian refused to give up Bryan, or worse, that he had killed him. Diana would take her anger out on me. I push my legs to my stomach, taking in a deep breath as the figure comes closer.

My eyes open when I feel a gentle touch, and Thalia's brown eyes meet mine.

"Mireya, we've got to work quick and get you out of here." She looks around and moves to grab an anvil and a hammer. I look at the handcuffs and shake my head when I realize her plan.

"You're going to have to trust me," she says and moves my hands so the chain connected to the handcuffs sits on the anvil. My hands shake and I close my eyes. Before I can suck in a breath, she slams the hammer down and the chain breaks. I release a cry and move to embrace her.

"Adrian," I manage to get out, and she pulls me forward.

"He was in the car behind me, but Julian had men running him down, so Axel and I came straight to you."

I look over to see Axel pulling out of the garage and driving around so the passenger doors face us. I hold on to Thalia as she moves us toward the car. Her right arm wraps around my waist, and her left hand holds a pistol in front of us. We're halfway there when I see more cars coming into view from the distance. Axel steps out and starts shooting at them with an assault rifle.

"GO BACK!" he screams, and Thalia drags me to the back of the shop. Gunshots continue to fire outside. Thalia pushes me behind a stack of tires and crouches down beside me, her gun pointed out in front of her.

The shots are becoming fewer and farther apart. I watch as Adrian steps in through the front door. He's covered in dirt and his white tank top is splattered with blood. When our eyes meet, I run towards him. He lifts me up, and I wrap my legs around him, sobbing into his neck.

"Just in time for the family reunion," I hear and look over Adrian's shoulder to see Diana exiting the office on the left end of the repair shop. She's holding a gun aimed at us. Thalia rushes toward her and she fires a shot, and

Thalia drops to the floor.

Axel storms inside and fires a shot to Diana's head, rushing to pick up Thalia.

"I'm okay. Just get them out of here." Thalia stands and holds her bleeding arm.

"We've got to get out of here. I can't find Julian." Axel and Thalia rush forward. Adrian picks me up, and I wrap my legs around him as he carries me. We make our way out through the back of the building, when I see a figure moving in toward us. Julian appears from the corner of my eye, aiming his gun at Adrian's back. I have no time to react. I reach for the gun in his waistband.

"ADRIAN!" I scream as the bullet rushes for us. Adrian drops us to the ground and another shot rings out. I watch as Julian's brains splatter in front of his body. I readjust my eyes and fall into complete shock when I see the person holding the gun behind Julian's lifeless body. My tia Vicky rushes toward me. I look to Adrian and cry out. He dropped in enough time to dodge the bullet Julian sent for us.

"Get her in the car now!" I watch as motorcycles fly down the hill toward us. Adrian throws us into the back seat and I cling to him. Axel and Thalia take the front seats as he speeds to the hospital.

"You're okay. Everything's okay." Adrian peppers me

with kisses and rubs my back. I cry into him. My eyes are heavy, and my body is exhausted. *He's okay.* I almost lost him, but he's okay. She heard me. La Santa Muerte heard me and spared his life. I close my eyes and let the tears flow freely in gratitude.

"Breathe, Mireya. You are here in this moment. You are safe, and you are cared for."

Chapter Thirty-Eight
Mireya

When I awake again, I see the white walls and smell that familiar scent. I'm lying in a hospital bed. I look around and find Adrian sleeping next to me. I'm okay. He's okay. I touch his face, and his eyes open.

"Diosa." He pulls me into him, kissing the top of my head, and I start to cry again. I swallow and my voice cracks. He has on a clean white undershirt, and I take in that familiar scent of jasmine and chrysanthemum.

"I thought I would never see you again."

He kisses my forehead, and he wipes the tears away. My body is trembling, and I can't stop. It's as if the wall I put up to hold it in all these years has broken and every hurt flows through, finally finding their own peace.

"I would never let anything happen to you." We lay there like that, embracing each other as we drift back to sleep. When the sun pours in through the windows, I open my eyes and take a moment to adjust to the light. I search for the clock. It's a little after seven in the morning, and I hear the sound of heels moving toward the door and a woman's voice.

Adrian must have set guards outside my room. I hadn't seen one nurse or doctor enter the room. I listen to the voices in the hall and recognize one.

"You will let me in this room immediately!" As I suspected, she gets her way, and I look up to see Tia Vicky walk through the door. Adrian jumps up right away and reaches for his gun.

"Tia," I say, pulling Adrian back. He lowers the weapon, and my tia gives him an ear to ear smile as she moves towards me.

"How are you doing, mija?" I start to cry again, and it's really out of my control at this point.

"I'm good. Just emotional," I say and wipe at the tears. I have never been so happy to see her. She's dressed more casually than yesterday. A black lace blouse and jeans. As beautiful as she has always been.

"It's the hormones, mija." She moves to grab my hand, and I look at Adrian. His face remains unphased. If he knows, he hasn't said anything. I haven't had time to tell him anything since he rescued me. And I'm not sure right now is a good time.

"Adrian, could you give me a moment alone with Mireya?"

"I'm not fucking leaving this room unless it's with her," he growls. I give him a glare, and she lets out a brief laugh.

"Very well." She walks to the side of the bed and reaches for me. She squeezes my hand, and I smile up at her. She had saved Adrian. The sight of Julian Nunez' brain splattering in front of me makes my stomach queasy, and I swallow down the bile rising.

"Mija, I am glad you are awake."

"What are you doing here?" I am more than happy to see her, but I'm not sure how she found out about everything. How she was there at the auto repair shop. For a moment, I thought I had dreamt it. She had always come to my every cry and call, but I had never imagined her shooting a man in cold blood the way she had.

"There are some things we need to discuss."

"Not now," Adrian growls and panic takes over me. Immediately, my hands move to my stomach.

"Is it the baby?"

"No. No. The baby is just fine." I sneak a quick glance at Adrian before I look back at her.

"Our baby is okay." His hand reaches to overlap mine on my stomach.

"But your mother is dead." I feel pressure in my chest. "Several men on motorcycles rode in and gunned her down. They took her body with them."

"I told you to wait!" Adrian stands, and my chest tightens. I zone their argument out and focus my mind on my mother. The way she threatened me at the apartment. The cruel and careless way she spoke to me.

"I'm so sorry, mija." She strokes my hair, and I search for the tears. I am still so angry at her. Sadness envelops me. I want to find a good memory to hold on to, but I can't. That doesn't mean I wanted her to die.

"Why would they do that?"

"I am assuming it was her son, Cassiel."

"Cassiel?" *My brother?* I had never heard the name. I never knew she had any children besides me.

"Our brother," Adrian interrupts, and my eyes search his.

They both began to fill me in on the events that had led to my mother's death. My mother had been another victim of Ivan Consuelo. A young girl, madly in love with a man who would use and extort her. She would carry his child and be forced to give the baby up to a kingpin, whose wife could not bear children, in exchange for an alliance.

"Did you know about him?" I look to Adrian, and he shakes his head.

"I had no idea."

"Did you?" I ask my tia, and she lets out a deep sigh.

"Not at first. When I met your mother, she was working at the hotel in Arizona. As soon as she found out my ex-husband and your father were a part of Los Peregrinos, she saw it as a way to find her son. She used Joaquin to find her way into the club. Joaquin was smarter than she thought, but when she got pregnant with you, she had something valuable to hang over his head. He loved you more than anything on this earth, Mireya." I knew my parents did not love each other. I saw how much my father put up with, the belittling and lack of love. She was cold, but he never seemed bothered by it. Now, I can see the sacrifices he made to stay close to me. He endured her hostility, as long as I was okay. It is sad to think he never experienced love the way he deserved.

"We didn't realize how far she was willing to go to find the child, but she had been stalking Ivan's every move. When she found out about Adrian, she became out of control. Hyper-obsessing over her son being the rightful heir to the Consuelo Legacy." I knew she disliked the Con-suelo family, but I summed it up to jealousy. It made sense now, her desperate need to mock and belittle the family. The lengths she went to hurt Adrian. The lengths she was willing to go to hurt my child.

"Do you know where he is? Cassiel?" I look to Adrian before I try to make sense of it. "Our brother?" There was someone out there–half me, half Adrian–and he was connected to us. He was our family. I couldn't help but worry about his life.

"Yes. But he does not want to be found, Mireya. He sent a message to her once, to warn her to stop looking for him, and her death was the final warning to all of us not to continue trying. He's dangerous."

He had her killed. The woman who had suffered in her attempts to find him had been killed in his name. He made a spectacle out of her death. While she had never been a good mother, she didn't deserve to die like that.

"Adrian, can you get me something to eat?" He looks at me, debating if he'll fight me on it, but I soften my eyes.

"I need to talk to my tia in private. As of today, she's all I have left."

He looks hurt, but gets up and walks to the door, looking back to check on me once more before exiting the room. My tia moves to the bed and hugs me tight.

"That man loves you." She runs her hand over my hair, the way she did when I was little.

"You think so?"

"Oh, I know so, mija. A man looked at me like that once, and I never forgot. Love like that is rare. You may not agree with his lifestyle, but he will always protect you and your baby." Her hand caresses my stomach.

"Do you know him?" I whisper, and she knows who I'm talking about. She stays quiet, searching my eyes, that are pleading with her to tell me about Cassiel. I, at least, deserve to know about the man who killed my mother. What if he is a threat to me and my child?

"In this life, you will need alliances, and those alliances are built from secrets. Secrets are the most powerful thing you can keep. I don't want to keep you from your brother, but he does not want to be found."

"Will he hurt me?"

"No. He will not harm you. He has his reasons for what he does, and I don't question him. Let him live his life, and he will let you live yours."

"She was going to kill my baby," I say, needing to get it off my chest. I know she's gone, but my tia had witnessed the way she emotionally broke me down. She presses her forehead to mine.

"It will be a cold day in Hell before I let anyone hurt you or this baby."

Chapter Thirty-Nine

Adrian

I exit the room, on the hunt for Dr. Aguilar and a cup of coffee. A cigarette would be nice, too, but I already got kicked out of one room. I don't need to get kicked out of the entire hospital.

As of today, she's all I have left.

I try not to take Mireya's words personally, but they eat at me. That lunatic in Prada heels is not the only person she has left. She has me, and I'm all she'll ever need. I will spend the rest of my life proving that to her.

When Diana kidnapped her, it felt like I was losing her all over again. When I brought her here, barely conscious, they ran tests and confirmed her pregnancy. I am more than happy. She had told me she was on birth control, but I don't care. If anything, there is a toxic part of me that needs her connected to me forever. We will form a family, and she will have me. Forever.

I see Dr. Aguilar leaving Thalia's room and stop him. "How is she?"

"She's doing well. Both she and Mireya are free to leave whenever they like." His tone is cold, but I thank him, anyway. I thought he was interested in Mireya for a while, but I have seen him around the hotel, frequenting Enrique's office, and I can put two and two together.

The door to Thalia's room is wide open, and she's sitting on the bed, her arm in a cast as she watches some telenovela on the hospital tv. She looks up when I walk in.

"Don't tell Enrique I'm doing this good. He'll make me go back to work." I roll my eyes.

"You ready to go back home?"

"Like forty-five minutes ago," she says, and we both laugh.

"Dr. Aguilar said Mireya can leave, too. When she's done talking to Vicky, I'll come for you, and we can leave together."

"That woman was a total badass! ¿No?"

"She's literally you in twenty-five years."

"I think that's the kindest thing you've ever said to me."

"What are we going to do about this long-lost brother of ours?"

"Fuck, Adrian. I'm on vacation right now. I don't want

to talk about work."

"You're in a fucking hospital bed because a psycho bitch shot you! This is not a vacation! We have another sibling out there!"

"He killed his biological mother just for attempting to find him. That's a pretty clear sign there's no family re-union in the near future." Her eyes are still on the tv, and I get up to pace the room, frustrated with her. Frustrated with everyone. I can't put Mireya in another situation where her life will be at risk. Where our baby's life will be at risk. Thalia looks up to me, pacing, and sighs.

"If he's not a threat, then we do nothing, Adrian. We deal with the bullshit we already have going on with Los Bandoleros, and we find the source of the creepy baby threats. You focus on Mireya and your baby. That's it!"

I nod in agreement. I have enough shit on my plate right now. I'm positive Los Bandoleros will become more aggressive the longer we hold their previous position. The gun business will be our ticket to expansion, and I have to be ready for multiple threats coming in. I don't have time to guess about my future. I know who I need in it, and that is enough. And I never want to see her in a hospital bed again. *Kill or be killed.*

I walk down to the cafeteria and grab a cup of coffee and some food for Mireya. I see Vicky exiting down the hall, so I walk in and set the food on the tray in front of her. It looks bland, and I notice Mireya's not interested either when I see the look on her face. I hate the smell of this place. Her wanting to have a career here makes no sense to me.

I need to get her home and into my bed and never let her leave, but I have a feeling tying her up would only excite her. I lean down and kiss her forehead. I want to scan every inch of her, make sure she's okay.

I walk to the window and look over the city. She stands up from the bed, and I rush to her, grabbing her waist.

"Be careful."

"I'm fine, Adrian. Are you?" She reaches up to touch my face gently, her fingers lingering. We stay there, our eyes locked, needing to touch one another. I trace the outline of the bruise left on her face.

"Dr. Aguilar told me we can leave whenever you're ready. Baby and you are okay."

She nods, but the look in her eyes is distant and sad.

"What's wrong?" There are a million things standing against us right now. She is trying to process it all, and I will give her all the time she needs. I hate to see her hurting, but I would have killed her mother myself for allowing this to happen to her.

"Mireya, look at me. You can talk to me."

"I didn't know how you were going to react to the baby. I barely had enough time to process it myself, but I want to keep it. I hope that's okay with you. I don't want you to feel stuck with me because I'm pregnant. We can co-parent—"

"Ya, ya." I press a finger to her lips to stop her ramblings. I move my hand to cup her face.

"There will be no fucking co-parenting or whatever the fuck you just said. I love you, Mireya. You are mine, and I am going to take care of you." I know she needs to hear that. She needs to know that I love her more than she can imagine. Since the first time I saw her, I knew she would be mine. I loved her then, and I will love her forever. We are meant to be together.

I would relive every fucked up scenario from my past, the feeling of abandonment, the loneliness that haunted me, and the nights of mental torture–all of it–if she would be waiting for me at the end of it.

She pulled that gun out of my jeans, ready to shoot Julian. She may not be Thalia, or some Queenpin, but she is far from weak. She will keep me grounded in the hard times and lift me up when the world tries to hold me down.

"This is my life, and it will be your life, too. It's violent, and it's messy, but I will always protect you. I will always make sure you are taken care of at any cost."

I grab her hands and rub my thumb over her wrists, over the gold chain bracelet and the red Santa Muerte bracelet that rest on her pulse.

"She saved me," she whispers, her head resting on my shoulder. "I thought I was going to die in there, and I called out to her to spare me from death, and she heard me."

I stare into her eyes and push back her hair behind her ear. Then I lean in and kiss her hard, my hands lost in the softness of her hair. She opens her mouth and lets me in. Our tongues meet, and I taste her sweetness. Her fists clench my shirt as she pulls me closer to her. We stay there, taking each other in. Letting the kiss sort through all the emotions we don't know how to talk through right now. Our bodies grind together, and our hands roam one another. She pushes me onto the bed and climbs on top of me.

"Damn. Slow down. Are you okay to do this right now?"

"I'm a nurse, Adrian, I'm fine. I'm also pregnant, emotional, and horny as hell."

"In that case, I think you need to be punished for what you said earlier." A smile grows on her face. I know what she needs. Both our emotions are high. I slide my hand under her hospital gown and cup her pussy.

"Adrian, let me lock the door. What if someone walks

in?" She bites her bottom lip, and my mouth moves to claim her lips as my own.

"Then they'll get one hell of a show." I pull the hospital gown over her head, and she lifts her arms. Her nipples are already hard. I pull one into my mouth and she shutters. I squeeze her bare ass, then I pull my hand back and slap it hard. She jumps, but her eyes let me know how much it excites her. My mouth marks her neck and chest. I bite her everywhere, just the way she likes.

"Tell me what you want, diosa." She doesn't shy away, as she pulls my erection out and wraps her hand around the base. She strokes it up and down while she stares at me. I watch as she spits on the tip and hiss as she takes the crown into her mouth.

She takes me down deep and sucks hard, stopping at the top to run her tongue over the sensitive tip. Her long hair spreads out all around me. I grab a fist full of it and push her down deeper. Spit gathers and leaks out the side of her mouth. I love the way her mouth feels, but I need more. I need to taste her arousal and swim inside her. I pull her off me by her hair as she catches her breath.

"Get on top and ride me." I rip off her panties and she bends forward, pressing her lips to my neck. I let my hand glide over her, feeling how wet she is. I stick my middle and ring finger into her and pull them out.

"You're soaking wet."

I move my fingers to my mouth and suck on her arousal before I shove them into her mouth. She closes her mouth around them and moans. My dick's so hard it hurts. When I remove them, she stares right into my eyes, and then slowly moves herself on top of me. She arches her back and places her hands behind her. The angle showing me her clit as she uses her ass to bounce on my cock. I rub my finger over her clit as I thrust into her from the bottom.

"Fuck me hard, Adrian."

I need to get in deeper. I move her so she's laying down and stand on the side of the bed, one of her legs on my shoulder and the other hanging off the side of the bed. I thrust in hard and she whimpers. I rub my finger over her sensitive nub, then pinch it hard. I grab her nipple and do the same.

"Who do you belong to?" I ask.

"I belong to you."

"Good girl." I pinch the other nipple, and her hands reach to hold tight to the bed's side rail. I thrust in hard and continue to play with her nipples.

"Cum all over me." I love when she talks dirty. Her wet pussy making that sweet symphony I like while I thrust into her. Her moans become longer and her breathing heavy. She's almost there. I pinch her clit one last time and she screams. Her orgasm breaks through, and I pound into her harder. My name never sounding sweeter. I want to cum all over her tits, but I'll wait till I get her home. I release myself inside her and slow my motions. I can't get enough of her. I want to stay inside her for a second longer, to feel the waves of her orgasm lower.

In our passion, I had forgotten where we were, and I remove myself from her so I can lock the door. "Really? Now you lock the door?" She rolls her eyes as she reaches to pull on her gown.

I move to her and bite down on her ass.

"I'm still not done punishing you for what you said."

"What did I say?" she asks as she stares back into my eyes. They are still full of lust, and if she's not careful, I'll take her for round two.

"You told your aunt that she is the only person you have left." She frowns and turns to look away. I pull her face back towards me.

"I am your family, too, now." My hand goes to rub her tummy. The life inside her. "Our family." I lower my lips to kiss the soft skin on her abdomen. In months to come, this stomach will grow and she will glow like the goddess she is. I feel her hand rub the back of my head as she looks down at me.

"I love you, Adrian."

"I love you, too, diosa. Let's go home."

Chapter Forty

Mireya

"To my family. My very reason for living," Don Vicente says, and everyone lifts their drink in unison. Thalia grabs my drink before I can take a sip and downs it. I laugh at her. It's been a few weeks since we were released from the hospital. Adrian took me back to his apartment, and I haven't left since. Alma decided to take a trip back to California, to see her foster parents, after having a rough time with me being kidnapped and the anniversary of her mom's death. I knew we'd have to have that uncomfortable talk about me moving out, but I didn't want to add to her stress.

Before I left the hospital, I made sure to stop by Thalia's room so I could thank her for coming for me that day. We were never the types for emotional apologies, and I'm sure any psychiatrist would say sweeping things under the rug was unhealthy, but our friendship would survive. I apologized for what I had said, but I didn't need to explain or interrogate her about the rumors. People often think friendship means sharing every single secret of your life, but if you really care for someone, you also respect their privacy on matters they are not willing to share with you.

She and Alma have been treating me like a porcelain doll since they found out I am pregnant. Not even Adrian has been that protective of me. I still haven't fully processed my mom's death, and both of them have been there for me every time the waves of grief come up.

Patricio met with the leader of Los Peregrinos to establish a peace treaty and retrieve my mother's body so I could hold a small ceremony for her. Gael helped me to find a therapist who could be trusted with the things I told her. She came from a family that was submerged in the cartel, and she has been able to not only relate, but also help me to process everything. My first session with Doctora Julia was last week, and it went well past the hour mark. I had admitted to her that my biggest fear was becoming my mother. There have been a lot of raw emotions. I find myself crying at the most random times. If I am this emotional this early in my pregnancy, I am afraid what I will be like in the months to come.

Adrian gives me that space to mourn my mother, despite

everything she did to him and his mother. He knows that there is a very human part of me that misses her. I miss the version of her that I hoped she would one day be. A healed version, who would apologize or praise me the way I desperately wanted her to.

I look up to see Adrian, standing with Adan and Osiel at the other end of the venue. He has on an all-black Brioni suit that outlines the masterpiece of his body. I spend most mornings watching him work out just so I can see that chiseled body. Adan and Adrian are both quiet by nature, so Osiel is the only one talking. Adrian holds a drink in his hand, but never takes his eyes off me.

"Stop staring," I mouth, and he flashes me a smile. The rare genuine one I have been seeing more frequently.

Everyone has come to celebrate Don Vicente. Soledad sits at a table with Patricio and Adriana. Adriana's husband is warm and charming. Conversations are never dry with his stories and sense of humor. Enrique and Doctor Aguilar sit with their friends. There is live music and people are laughing and dancing.

Most of the room is watching as Ariella graces some man with the gift of dancing with her. She has not sat down since she arrived. Every time she moves to sit, another guy is asking her to dance. Each one tries to outdo the next with exaggerated dips and turns. She keeps up with every spin, her high heels gliding on the floor in perfect sync.

Her bodyguard holds Guapo at the table reserved for her and her brothers. The poor man looks like he is being tortured. The ugly dog sleeps in his arms. Axel is also on the dance floor, and I am wondering if each of the Reyes children has had private dance lessons, because even the few times Thalia dragged Adan out, he was an excellent dancer. Everyone is watching the Reyes siblings dance the night away, but I am staring back at Adrian.

He looks so handsome in a suit, his tattoos visible on his hands and neck. This pregnancy has me desperate for him to take me at any minute.

Adrian in a white tee. *I'm Feral!*

Adrian working out on the patio. *I'm Feral!*

Adrian in a suit. *Feral! Feral! Feral!*

The constant need to devour this man and let him claim me is unreal. Even before we left the hotel, I begged him to fuck me on the kitchen table. Looking at him, I realize something: it's easy to love someone when you are lonely. When you are by yourself with nothing to hold on to, your mind will wander to the thought of them. Missing them. But Adrian and I can be in a crowd full of people and miss each other. Mere feet feel like miles to me right now. Some might say this is toxic, and I would agree. I'll take toxic love over fake love. He sees all my flaws and loves me, anyway.

I know his dark side, and I am willing to embrace it rather than run from it.

The band stops for a break, and the DJ takes over. "Oceans" by Karol G and Jessie Reyes comes on, and I watch as Adrian makes his way toward me. Adrian is not a fan of Regional Mexican music; he also dislikes Reggaeton, and he disgraces the entire state of Texas by refusing to listen to any country. I was sure he would not ask me to dance all night, so I'm surprised when he reaches out for my hand and moves me to the dance floor.

Adriana made a girls' date out of dress shopping a few days ago and took Thalia, Ariella, myself, and even Soledad. Soledad and I felt awkward in the luxurious boutique, but Adriana made the experience comfortable with her hospitality towards us. She is humble, despite her fortune.

"Patricio will pay for all of this. Buy whatever you want," she had said, and Thalia laughed harder than all of us. Adriana and Patricio bickered the same way Thalia and Adrian did. They protected one another with the same fierceness, too. It's hard not to think of Cassiel when I see their sibling bonds.

I had settled on a glittery champagne backless gown, and Ariella helped me with my hair and makeup. Loose curls frame my face.

"You look so beautiful," Adrian says as he pulls me up and walks me to the dance floor. I wrap my arms around him and we sway to the music. He pulls back slightly and brings my hand to his lips, pressing a gentle kiss to it.

"What are you thinking, diosa?" he whispers into my ear.

"I'm thinking about how I could get used to seeing you in a suit."

"I'm thinking this dress is too tight, and I am going to have to kill every man who is looking at you."

"Do you ever not think of violence?"

"Not when it comes to you." He looks at me and smiles. His classic mischievous grin. For a second, I think he'll pick me up and move me to the penthouse to fuck me out of this dress. Instead, he moves back and lets go of me. He reaches into his pocket, and I almost lose my breath as I watch him drop to his knee.

The music fades out, and I can feel every eye on me. Adrian hates public displays of affection, which was great for my anxiety. Right now, I feel like I may pass out.

"Diosa, look at me." I look down and meet his beautiful brown eyes. He slips a ring onto my finger. 18k white gold with an emerald-cut diamond. I don't know much about designer brands, but I know jewelry.

"You are the only thing that brings me to my knees. Will

you let me worship you for the rest of our lives?" I don't have to even think about it before I am saying, 'Yes,' and he stands to kiss me as the crowd cheers. I would live this life and every one after with Adrian. He would always be mine.

Epilogue One

Adrian

Patricio helps me to unload the last box from the penthouse. After considering our future, I decided the safest place for my family was here, on Patricio's estate, with him, my mom, my grandfather, and his security team. There would be nights when I didn't come home, and Mireya knew that. It was a part of the life I chose, and this was how I would secure her safety.

The house Patricio had been building for me was similar to his hacienda-designed mansion. Three levels and five large bedrooms, with plenty of living and dining space. When I brought Mireya here, she instantly fell in love with it. She has spent every night since looking up décor and asking for my input.

Thalia is helping me to invest the money I've made, and my inheritance, into other streams of income and stocks. Mireya almost passed out when I gave her her very own AmEx Black card. We both are adjusting to this lifestyle. We had spent our whole lives trying not to overspend the little we had, to being able to afford indulgences and trying not to feel guilty for it. I walk through the back room of the house to the master bedroom and see a crib already set up.

"I hope it's okay," Patricio says from behind me. "I wanted to get it for the baby, but you can move it or I can take it back."

"No. It's perfect." A tightness pulls in my chest. I'm still not sure how I fit into this family, but I know my child will be surrounded by love. My mother has been clean for nine months and is thriving in her sobriety. She spends most of her time helping Don Vicente in his garden, and has made it her personal mission to make sure Mireya is cared for. She wasn't the mother I needed her to be when I was younger, but I am happy to give her the opportunity to be a loving grandmother to my child.

Patricio starts to walk back to the moving truck.

"Thank you," I say, and he turns to look at me.

"Not just for the crib... for everything." He smiles for a

moment, then nods and turns away again. I have to pick up Mireya from the hospital, so I walk to my grandfather's house to pick up the engagement gift he had given me a few days ago. I want to surprise her with it.

When I get to the front of the hospital, I see Mireya walking out. She has been coming here for her practicum with Dr. Aguilar. She doesn't see me at first, but I knew she wouldn't recognize me in my grandfather's Impala. He had it painted green for me, and I requested he put on gold rims.

I whistle, and Mireya turns to give me a dirty look. *Good girl.* That's exactly what she should do if a man whistles at her. Her skin is glowing, and I smile at the small bump that hides behind her scrubs. When she notices it's me, her eyes soften, and she walks towards me. "Adrian. How did you convince Don Vicente to let you drive Lola?"

"Lola is ours now." Her eyes light up as she slides in, and I pull her in for a kiss.

"Thanks to you, diosa." I reach to touch her belly where my son is growing. "You are carrying his very first great-grandson, so I guess you're kind of special."

"Ugh, more like bloated, with Godzilla ankles, but special sounds better."

I laugh and take the long way home, so we can cruise for a bit. She moves her hand out the window, smiling as the wind beats against her open palm.

"I think I want to be a midwife." She can read the confusion on my face. I have no fucking idea what a midwife is.

"It's like a gynecologist. I would help other women through pregnancy and giving birth."

"You want to stare at vaginas for a living?" I would one-hundred percent support that. I wouldn't have to worry about some guy hitting on her if she was staring at vaginas all day. She hits me on the shoulder.

"No, I want to help women have a more comfortable experience giving birth in the comfort of their home."

"I would much rather you be a gina-cologist than touch any other man again."

"It's gynecologist." She laughs, and I still don't hear the difference.

"Whatever makes you happy, diosa."

And I mean that. A younger version of myself would sacrifice for her just so she could follow her dreams. Now, I will just work harder to make sure nothing is out of her reach. She belongs to me, and I belong to her. We would build a home out of the house Patricio had built for us. We would fill it with children and give them the love we never received as children.

The life I live doesn't always guarantee a tomorrow, but

I'll take every opportunity to celebrate her and her dreams. She is my whole world.

Epilogue Two

Mireya

5 YEARS LATER

Adrian is chasing PJ down the hill to the cemetery.

"Welo! Welo!" PJ says and runs straight to Patricio.

Patricio picks him up and hugs him. We came here to clean up Vicente's grave before Dia de Los Muertos. Adrian kisses his mom and shakes Patricio's hand when we reach them.

"Adrian, you made her walk all this way. Look at her feet!" Soledad says and reaches in for a tight hug.

I look down at my swollen feet. Our baby girl is due any day now. Adrian smirks at me.

"That's her punishment. This is what happens when she can't keep her hands off me." I roll my eyes. Patricio has already taken off down the hill with PJ, chasing him as he laughs. It warms my heart. Patricio and Adrian had a rough start–shit, we all did–but Patricio has proven himself time and time again. Adrian and I had made a bet that if the baby was a girl, I would pick the first name and him the middle, but if it was a boy, he could pick the first name. When we found out we were having a boy, I already knew I was going to put Joaquin as the middle name for my father.

Adrian had gone back and forth between names... most of them were horrible. Al Pachino or Vito Corleone I immediately shot down. When I went into labor, I couldn't get ahold of Adrian, and Patricio was there to take me to the hospital. He was always there. Looking back from the beginning, his love for Soledad outshone anything else he ever cared about. He gave us a home, he found Soledad, and he brought me to Adrian. I know that's why Adrian chose Patricio as our son's first name. Even if he does get jealous that PJ wants to stay at Welo's house every weekend and tells everyone at preschool that Patricio is in the Avengers.

Adrian runs and scoops PJ up and moves him around like an airplane. He slows down to wait for me, and PJ takes right back off to catch Patricio and Soledad. Watching Adrian as a husband and father makes me wish I had more time with my dad.

The role of a father or grandfather is an important role. Whether it be bound by blood or not. I often think of the brief time I got to spend with mine and wonder if he would be proud of me. If he saw me where I was, would he agree with my life choices? I'm not always sure I am, to be honest, but life holds so many surprises. Different paths and obstacles of sacrifice and gain. Through it all, I look back and realize as long as I ended up here with Adrian and my children, I am happy.

I catch up to him and he reaches for my hand.

"Diosa, you sure you don't want to go home? We can clean this up."

"No. I want to be here. I loved Don Vicente as much as you did." He nods and grabs my hand. Losing Don Vicente was one of the hardest days of our married lives. I held him that night as he held back the tears. I held his hand through the difficult funeral. While nothing was eternal, I knew the name and legacy Don Vicente left behind for his grandchildren would live on.

We both watch as PJ holds tight to Patricio, who holds him in his left arm while holding Soledad's hand in his right.

I look at Adrian, remembering a time I was afraid of him coming home, and now, he is my home. As if he can read my thoughts, his thumb rubs over my bracelets, and then he brings them to his lips. Many of them are rare and of value, but none are as special as the first one he gave me.

A gentle kiss and a soft whisper, "I love you."

Acknowledgments

Thank you for reading my debut novel. I would copy and paste Snoop Dogg's entire speech, but I think it's okay to sum it up by saying I wanna thank me, for never quitting. The imposter syndrome got heavier the closer I got to releasing this book. It can be scary trying something new but writing has always been my safe place. I am grateful for the process and I hope along the way this encourages you to fight for what you want.

Thank you to my sister who listened to the idea and became my first cheerleader. My kids and husband who dealt with me in writing mode for months on end. My friends Sam and Gabi, I hope you find yourself scattered someway throughout my books. There were many countless nights we laughed our asses off at the Frontier and I made you retell stories while I sat there like blues clues taking notes on my phone. I honor your hoe days.

Desiree, thank you for always staying connected to me through the years. You're random intuitive check in calls always came on days I needed your encouragement the most. Thank you for helping me find Adrian's back for the cover.

To my entire family. My brothers answering some of my weirdest questions. My grandma. Really my grandma is reading this ya'll. Between my grandma's Danielle Steel two spice smut to my mom filling her house with VC Andrews, I was only destined to travel this Dark Romance path. I'm still laughing about the day I asked my mom if she would be embarrassed about the sex scenes I wrote and she said "No, I'll tell people you interviewed me for inspiration before writing them." You're the best mom.

My editor Sarah at Indie Proofreading, you were the biggest sign the universe could send me to push this along. You are an amazing editor, and I was saving my virginity for you. Thank you so much for walking me through this journey and answering all my questions.

I hate that I might forget some people but just know I'm grateful for everyone who paved a path for me. There are countless people who have supported me from within the social media community, and in real life. All of you have touched my life in some way or another. Just the fact you have this book in your hands means that you believe in me. Thank you.

Contact Me

Nix's Toxicas: This is a spoiler room on Facebook where others can discuss this book as well as future books. I will be reaching out about street teams, and future ARC readers through this interactive group.

Follow my other accounts for upcoming news:

Facebook Page: Author Nix Murguia

Instagram: @Calaverahotels & @hauntgirlnix_

Tiktok: @hauntgirlnixx

Website: https://hauntgirlnix.com/

Thalia & Silas

Book 2 of Calavera Hotels

Coming Fall 2024